THE
ROAD
NOT
TAKEN

THE ROAD NOT TAKEN

SAM LAMB

atmosphere press

© 2025 Sam Lamb

Published by Atmosphere Press

Cover design by Matthew Fielder

Cowboy boot icon by Iuliia Soloveva from vecteezy.com

No part of this book may be reproduced without permission from the author except in brief quotations and in reviews. This is a work of fiction, and any resemblance to real places, persons, or events is entirely coincidental.

Atmospherepress.com

This story is dedicated to Larry...
whatever road you've taken.

I shall be telling this with a sigh
Somewhere ages and ages hence:
Two roads diverged in a wood, and I—
I took the one less traveled by,
And that has made all the difference.

From the poem "The Road Not Taken"
by Robert Frost

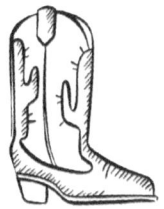

CHAPTER 1

He watched her from his corner stool at the bar. He'd been watching her for three consecutive Friday nights. He was positive it was the same girl in the picture his uncle had given him. She didn't drink as much as her dark-haired girlfriend, who looked like a lot of fun. More his kind of girl. But he had specific instructions about the girl in the photograph. He was debating if he should make his move tonight or wait another week. The pull to go back to Montana was strong. And he knew that work was piling up back home.

He saw her friend order another round of drinks, and when the waitress looked his way, the debate was settled. After he was served the drink, compliments of the brunette, he made his way to their table.

Her name was Lucy. And she was obviously interested. Jack was tempted, but bedding Lucy was not his goal. He was on a mission. Over the last three Fridays, Jack had already turned down a number of girls in his search for *this girl*—Lucy's friend—the one in the photograph he'd been given. It had taken longer than Jack expected to find her, and he could not afford to be distracted now that he was so close. JT was pushing for a progress report, and JT was not a patient man. But

Jack was. He already knew this girl's name, of course, but he waited to see if Lucy would introduce him. After all, orchestrating this "chance encounter" was just part of the game.

There were now six people crowded around two very small, round tables set in front of a long bench that stretched the length of the bar. They were lucky enough to have some chairs too. Every round table down the length of the bench was occupied. Those not so lucky to have snagged a table were packed into the space between them and the bar.

The entire joint was dimly lit, darkly paneled, loud, and crowded with college students blowing off steam. And if this Friday was like the others Jack had endured, the bar would get even more crowded once the band started playing. There was a decent-sized dance floor in front of the staging area for the band. He knew this college town in the middle of the cornfields boasted five bars, each one with a different atmosphere. The one next door had a huge dance floor under a mirrored ball that played disco. This bar played more country music and Jack silently thanked the fates for that.

The girl in the photo had her head bent, trying to listen over the noise to the boy talking to her. The boy was saying something about a discussion in a class they attended together. He was doing most of the talking, while the girl nodded occasionally. Jack caught pieces of the conversation while simultaneously answering questions from Lucy.

Finally, from close up, Jack could study the girl. Her hair was an unusual shade of reddish blonde. Even seated, he could tell she was tall and slender. He imagined the wicked things she could do with those long legs.

Occasionally Jack would catch the girl looking at *him* and he would try to maintain longer eye contact. In front of her was a half-full glass of beer and an untouched shot of some clear liquor. She didn't appear to be getting drunk. Not like Lucy, who was moving past friendly to seductive.

I met him in a college bar where we were prematurely celebrating the end of the semester and graduation. It was only fall midterms, so we still had another semester before graduating. It was the crazy, wild, sexually free, burn-your-bra, women's-lib seventies. Nixon was President. Woodstock was a memory, birth control pills were a reality, and marijuana—well, it was everybody's pipe dream.

For mid-October, the weather was still mild. If not for the rustle of fallen leaves, you might think it was spring. At least if it had been spring, that would explain how it happened. If spring could turn a young man's thoughts to love, it could certainly do the same thing for a young woman.

I was not attracted to him in the bar. I had noticed him, sitting in the corner, like a big, dark, hairy spider, waiting for his prey to stumble by. He was not my type, if I even *had* a type. But as he accepted Lucy's free drink, joined our group, and sat down near me, I experienced a funny tingle.

It was unnerving when his startling blue eyes locked onto mine. Several times I had to look down at my drink or at my classmate still defending the argument he lost in class. I had to admire him for that. He *could* be my type: a fair-haired, clean-shaven boy. But I didn't feel anything else for him, even though I knew he was interested in something more.

Lucy was a wild one. On Friday nights, when we would go to the bars on the main drag of the small midwestern college town, she would start off drinking beer and end the evening slamming back shots. Short, no taller than five-foot-four, Lucy had beautiful, thick, dark brown hair and the warmest olive-toned skin that tanned naturally in a few hours of sun. She was borderline plump and she would never win a beauty pageant, but she had a contagious party-going personality that more than compensated for her looks. Wherever she went, her outgoing nature and raucous behavior soon drew an entourage. She made friends easily and people liked her. They delighted in—as well as encouraged—Lucy's outrageous behavior. She amazed me with how she could gather so many admirers week after week and enjoy weekend after weekend of one-night stands. I wasn't a prude, nor was I still a virgin. But the few experiences I had between the sheets weren't encouraging me to look for more.

I was almost Lucy's polar opposite. My hair was strawberry blonde and worn long, as was the fashion at the time, and I had a fair complexion that sunburned easily. I was tall and slim; some might say skinny. But I once overheard some girls in the locker room, not realizing I was in there, wishing they had my slender frame.

One girl said, "I'll bet she can wear just about anything and it'll look good on her."

"And she never has to have anything hemmed," added the other girl.

At the time, I just smiled to myself because they were right.

I was Lucy's opposite in personality too. I was quiet, more introspective, and rarely did shots or engaged in outrageous actions. Most of the boys found me standoffish. But it was really shyness on my part rather than snobbery. I envied girls like Lucy who could be so free to just...let go.

Lucy was obviously interested in the attractive stranger, so I thought no further about investigating the cause of the tingle. Besides, it was difficult to have any kind of conversation in the noisy bar. I pretended to listen politely to the fellow from my class, but I was actually trying to hear the newcomer's answers to Lucy's questions.

"I'm Lucy and I love to party!" Exaggerating *love* and *party*, making it sound like a sexy invitation. *She can't help herself.*

"Jack," he told her with a clink of his glass to hers.

"Do you go to school here?" Lucy continued.

Not a student. He's older. Maybe a professor? But they didn't usually hang out at the bars.

"No. I'm here visiting my uncle," he said.

"Where's home, Jack?" Lucy continued her flirting.

Not from around here. He was wearing cowboy boots.

His voice dropped and the volume of the band went up. I think he said Montana. On a farm. Or a ranch.

I studied him as they talked. He was a big guy. Not fat, but solid. I'm terrible at guessing heights, but I'd say at least six feet, maybe a few inches more. He had thick black hair that brushed the collar of his shirt. And a dark, stubbly beard. Like he hadn't shaved for several days. I thought he looked a bit like a Neanderthal and briefly fantasized about being thrown over his shoulder and taken to his cave. I shook my head to erase that image. *No, he's not my type at all.*

But Jack had a raw sensuality about him that was difficult to ignore, and he would occasionally send me *that* look, with the bluest of eyes, that made me shiver. I knew Lucy would be attracted to this bad boy. *And she can have him. He'll be nothing but trouble.*

The band started playing and that ended any further eavesdropping. Lucy tried to get Jack to dance but he waved her off. Jack tried to ask me something across the table but I just shook my head. It was impossible to hear over the loud music.

The band played several sets. More pitchers of beer were bought and emptied. More shots were chugged. I danced a couple of times with the boy from my class.

Lucy danced with everyone, it seemed—except Jack, who, I guessed, just didn't dance. *Maybe it was the boots.* By now, Lucy had accumulated quite a few followers. The bar was closing soon and I wondered if Lucy would have her "after-the-bars-closed" party.

The bartender shouted "LAST CALL," the lights came up,

and the collective reaction to the sudden glare was audible. Lucy started telling folks her address, and then she invited Jack back for the party.

~~~~~~

Jack wasn't positive the girl in the photo would be at Lucy's party. But they appeared to be friends and the address was on the way back to his uncle's house, so he decided to chance it. He really needed to move his mission along. Tomorrow he'd have to talk to JT and he wanted to report that he was making progress. This wasn't his usual style, chasing a girl. In Montana, women mostly threw themselves at him. He'd had his pick. Once he'd had Cathy, though, the others never had a chance. But it didn't help to stir up his thoughts, and his dick, thinking about Cathy.

He walked to Lucy's apartment. He'd have to let her know he wasn't interested. He had hoped not dancing with her might be enough, but by accepting the invitation to her apartment, he feared that would send the wrong message. He followed her instructions and went around to the back of the building and, with a sigh, knocked on the door of Apartment Number 4.

~~~~~~

There were already about ten fairly inebriated students at the party when Jack arrived. He handed a six-pack to Lucy. I watched her stash it with the others already in the cooler by the back door. *Just what we need, more beer.* Lucy had loud party music playing in another room, but most folks were still standing in the kitchen, close to the beer supply. I knew later, the volume, as well as the tempo, would mellow as the party progressed.

To my surprise, Jack sought me out and stayed close. A couple of times, I caught a funny look from Lucy, who had probably thought, since Jack showed up, that he would hang out with her. But she didn't act overly upset as there were at least two other guys who were obviously interested in her.

Jack had maneuvered me into an empty space in the hallway. We both started to say something at the same time.

"Go ahead," I said, although I thought ladies should go first.

He introduced himself. "My name is Jackson Juddson."

How alliterative, I thought, smiling to myself.

"My full name is Jackson *Lawrence* Juddson, but some of my friends do call me JJ," he added, as if he noticed my smile and knew what I was thinking. "Most folks call me Jack."

"Well, I'm Elizabeth Sarah Mitchell. Lucy calls me Liz. She is the *only* one I let call me that. My mother always called me Elizabeth. As do most of my classmates."

"What are you studying, Beth?"

The look on my face must have prompted him to explain. "I like Beth," Jackson announced. "You'll be Beth to me."

I should have said something right then, but he gave me that look, again, with those wickedly beautiful eyes. So that was that. *I guess I'm Beth now.*

"So, what *are* you studying?" he asked again.

This was a bit of a sore subject for me, but looking him straight in those blue eyes, I told him, "I'm an English major, *Jackson*. With an emphasis on Literature."

It was a prickly subject because every advisor warned me that I wouldn't find a teaching job. There were too many English teachers in the market.

"I'm not sure if I'll teach or go on to graduate school," I continued. *Grad school is just postponing the inevitable. I'll have to find another career. Or a husband.* "How about you? College?"

"Yes, I have a degree in agriculture from Montana State in Bozeman."

"What do you do in Montana, Jackson?"

He raised an eyebrow at the second use of Jack*son*. "I work on a ranch. Cattle mostly. Some horses. And lots of hay."

I had no frame of reference for this type of work and didn't quite know what to ask next. Lucky for me, folks were migrating down the hall toward the music.

The party had thinned to five or six hearty partiers, and we all moved to the living room. Someone lit a joint and passed it around. I took a small toke to be polite and passed it to Jackson. He took a couple of hits and passed it on. Inevitably, I got sleepy. It looked like Lucy would be safe with the few folks remaining. I stood to leave and Jackson asked if he could walk me home.

I chuckled. "Sure. But it's a very short walk. I live right next door."

He followed me out of Lucy's apartment and into the front foyer of the building. I had my key out and was planning on making a fast entrance into my apartment. It had been a long day, a longer evening, and I was tired. But Jackson didn't seem to want the evening to end. I think he was expecting me to invite him in.

"I don't do one-night stands," I told him bluntly. "If you're looking for that, I suggest you go back next door."

For a brief moment—it could have been my imagination—I thought I caught a flare of irritation, like fire in water, in his eyes.

"I'd like to see you tomorrow," Jackson told me.

It was my turn to look startled. "Well, it already *is* tomorrow," I quipped.

With a smirk, he volleyed back, "Okay, then how about later *today*? Dinner? What's your favorite restaurant?" Before I could answer, Jackson told me, "I'll pick you up at seven and you can tell me then."

"Wait," I said as he turned to go out the door. "I'll meet you there. Do you know Dos Machos, on the main street, across from the pond?"

He looked like he was going to argue about the arrangements, but with a satisfied grin, he said, "I'll find it. I'll see you there at seven. 'Til tonight."

I knew with just a smidge of encouragement, he would lean in and kiss me. I reminded myself that I was not attracted to his dark looks nor impressed with his assertive manner, so I slipped into my apartment as he went out the front door.

~~~~~~

As he walked the few blocks to his uncle's house, Jack was pleased she'd agreed to have dinner with him. Of course, she might have said yes just to get him to leave. And then she might not show at the restaurant. But something told him she would. Well, he hoped she would. He'd at least be able to tell JT that contact had been made and things were moving along. Get the old man off his case. And wouldn't he think it a hoot that she'd called him Jackson? She had some spunk. This would be more fun than he'd imagined.

With that settled, his thoughts again turned to Cathy and how soon he could get back to Montana. He missed the smell of horses and hay. He'd been in this college town now for three weeks. He was tired of it. He'd done crowded college bars and late-night parties. He needed open spaces and the mountains. And his dick sure could use some attention from Cathy.

CHAPTER 2

I slept in later than usual. After some coffee and a light breakfast, I straightened up the apartment. By then, I heard Lucy's music next door, so I went over to see how the party ended. She had gotten *lucky*, as she put it, but he had left soon after, which was fine with her. She preferred sleeping alone and sometimes it was awkward for her if the guy wanted to stay. Knowing Lucy, she would be on the prowl for a new conquest soon enough.

"So. Tell. What happened with Jack last night?" Lucy teased.

"Nothing. I went in my apartment and he went out the door," I told her.

"So that's it? You won't see him again?" Lucy asked.

"I'm supposed to meet him at Dos Machos tonight at seven. But I haven't decided whether I'll go or not," I confessed.

"Well, Liz, he does know where you live. Won't he just show up here if you don't show?"

"Probably. He's kind of pushy."

"How so?" Lucy wanted to know.

I didn't want to tell her about how he had decided to call me Beth and I did nothing to stop him. Or how he had *told* me he'd pick me up. Didn't ask.

"I don't know. Just a feeling I got. There is *something* about him, right?" I asked, changing the subject.

"You bet, Liz. He's hot. Did you notice his eyes? Such a startling shade of blue."

"I'm sure you think he's hot. He's definitely more your type than mine. That black-haired bad-boy type."

"Uh-huh. Who knows, Liz, maybe you'll marry him, move to Montana, and have a bunch of kids," Lucy said with mischief—or was it jealousy?—in her eye.

I shuddered. *That's never gonna happen. I'll have dinner with him and that's it.*

"It's a free dinner, Lucy. At my favorite place. Come over later and help me pick out something to wear," I invited.

~~~~~~

I studied some in the afternoon, and napped some as well. I had a semester and a half left and was struggling with what I'd do after that. I hated to believe the advisors about not finding a job after graduation. I'd wanted to teach high school literature ever since I fell in love with books. Reading has taken me to places I'll never visit in person. To introduce that kind of traveling to young people would be my dream job.

I so envied Lucy. She was graduating in the spring as well, but she had already been accepted to graduate school in Arizona for the fall semester. She knew exactly what she wanted to do: teach deaf students. And special ed teachers were in demand. Not so for English Lit teachers. I was pretty much adrift. Some days I toyed with the idea of graduate school. But in what field? Continue on in Literature or go an entirely different direction?

I was pretty much on my own. I was an only child. My father had died when I was really young. Or left. I wasn't really sure. Mom always said he was dead, but I wondered. If there were any pictures of him, Mom never shared them with me. From time to time, I would ask Mom about my father, but I would always get vague answers.

"He was a good man," she told me once.

Another time, she said, "I truly loved that man."

A few years ago, I asked again.

"Elizabeth, that was a long time ago and I really can't remember."

I could see that the memories were painful, so I dropped it. I didn't want her to think that having one wonderful parent wasn't enough.

Mom had a sister, but she died long before I was born. She had no children. So, I had no cousins.

Mom's dream was for me to go to college and get a degree. But in my junior year, she died suddenly. I didn't know she was sick and neither did she, apparently. The cancer consumed her quickly and let her linger between painful consciousness and sweet oblivion for ten days.

I briefly wondered what Mom would think of Jackson and his decision to call me Beth. She *always* called me Elizabeth. She told me once that a person's name is the most important thing they have.

After her funeral, I cleaned out her apartment. She didn't have much. Besides the furniture and the dishes, there was some clothing and a few pieces of jewelry I kept. I cherished her wooden recipe box. It was comforting to see her handwriting on the stained recipe cards. And there was a small metal strongbox that held important papers. I found the key amidst the jewelry, and after a quick cursory look, I vowed to go through the papers when I got back to campus. But the locked box got shoved into the back of my closet when I returned to school, and it has remained unopened ever since. There would be time to go through the papers later. Until then, I avoided the contents, believing whatever was in that box might be too painful to discover.

I packed up the things I wanted and donated the rest. The landlord was gracious about the lease as Mom was a good tenant, always paying the rent early and not causing any fuss. She did leave me some money, and there was a small insurance policy. It was enough to finish school and then some, to either go on to graduate school or relocate somewhere for a job. Or even take a year off.

~~~~~~

Lucy came over later in the afternoon and we went through my closet to find an outfit.

"Liz, I like the white lacy peasant blouse," Lucy decided after the bed had accumulated a pile of tops.

That one had long, lace-trimmed sleeves with more lace around the open neckline and a fake drawstring tie closing a three-inch slit. Virginal but sexy at the same time.

"Just don't get the sleeves in the guacamole," Lucy advised.

The jeans were easy. We both agreed on my favorite pair.

I was tall: five-foot-eight. Probably tall enough to be a model, but that career had never held any appeal. My long hair was worn in the seventies hippie parted-down-the-middle style. I had a trim figure, still taut in all the right places. In addition to walking all over campus, I swam several times a week in the university pool to keep it that way. I complained often to my mother about my small breasts, but she had always countered with a compliment on my cute little butt. My jeans tended to highlight that feature. Especially my favorite ones. They fit like a glove.

"I wish I had your boobs, Lucy," I sighed.

"Well, *I* wish I had *your* butt," she remarked.

"Should we get in a bag, jump up and down, and see if we can mix up the parts?" I chuckled.

"It'd be easier if it worked like a Mr. Potato Head," she laughed.

~~~~~~

The day dragged for Jack. There wasn't much to do at his uncle's house. He couldn't get interested in any of the college football games on TV. His thoughts continually drifted to Montana and Cathy. He sure did miss her and her sassy ways. How was he ever going to make this work?

Well, first things first, he told himself.

~~~~~~

I drove the few blocks to Dos Machos a few minutes before seven. As college towns go, this one was small and compact. The college buildings were all on one side of town and the restaurants and bars on the other. Go a few miles in any direction and you'd be in the cornfields.

Dos Machos was *the* local Mexican restaurant. Family-owned, it served fairly authentic Tex-Mex food in a casual atmosphere.

Jackson was already seated at a corner table when I walked in. He stood up to get my attention, but it was unnecessary. Between his height and his good looks, he was impossible to miss. As I walked to the table, I could see other girls' heads turn to stare at Jackson. I chuckled to myself. *Yep, he has that effect. "Heartbreaker" written all over him.* Again, I wondered what I was doing here. He wasn't my type, yet there was *something*. Like a magnet to steel, against my will, I was being pulled in.

I was glad he had arrived first, so I didn't have to feel

self-conscious waiting for him. And this spared me from sitting there and wondering whether *he* would show.

"I was hoping you weren't going to stand me up, darlin'. But of course, I do know where you live. And then I'd just hafta come hunt you down."

Not only did my heart stop, but I was also rendered speechless. He had a way of saying *darlin'* that would melt glaciers. Hearing him call me that in his sexy undertone, then his admission of wondering if *I'd* show, threatening to "hunt me down" just like Lucy said he would, and all delivered with that piercing stare. Oh, the man had a way about him. Luckily, I was saved by the appearance of the waitress to take our drink orders.

Jackson asked, "Beth, do you like tequila?"

"Yes," I managed to murmur.

He ordered margaritas for us both and a nacho appetizer.

Before I could fully recover, he took my hand and told me in that same sexy manner, "Beth, you look ravishing."

What? Like good enough to eat? I couldn't tell if he meant "ravishing" as an adjective or a verb.

"Oh, I'll bet you say that to all the girls in Montana," I teased, trying to recover my poise. "And tell me, does it work?" I extracted my hand from his.

"Does it work for what, darlin'?"

Damn the man. Did he know that every time he said *darlin'* in that sultry voice, it caused a flutter below my belly button? I'll just bet he did.

Still flustered and having lost the flow of the flirtation, I changed tactics and turned the conversation to a safer subject. "Tell me about Montana. I've lived in this area all my life so I don't really know much about that part of the country."

I'd evidently hit on a good subject as Jackson proceeded to entertain me with information about his home state.

"Montana is the fourth largest state and has the nickname

'The Treasure State,'" he bragged.

"I remember from some geography class it's called 'Big Sky Country,' but how'd it get that other nickname?" I inquired.

"Well, darlin', it's because I live there."

I laughed out loud at this and he winked at me. As we sipped margaritas and munched on nachos, he told me more about Montana and I studied him as he talked. I could tell this evening, even in the fading light of the restaurant, that he was definitely older. We hadn't exchanged those vital statistics yet, but I was guessing he was in his mid to late twenties. He had the most unusual shade of blue eyes I'd ever seen, with a row of crinkles at the outside corners. The rest of his face was unlined but tanned. And that beard. Really more like a heavy five o'clock shadow that made me want to reach out and touch it to see if it was soft or stubbly. And of course, his size. Big. No, probably large. I could just hear Lucy wondering out loud if everything on this tall stranger was big. Or large.

I brought myself back to the conversation. I could hear the pride in his voice when he told me that Montana was one of the largest states, only smaller than Alaska and Texas, and, oh, just slightly smaller than California, like that state didn't really count. And then, I heard the humor in his voice when he said the cattle population outnumbered the people population.

"And we have grizzly bears, which is a problem for our ranch. Every year, we have to kill one or two. Hate to do it, but once they discover the easy pickings of our cattle, we can't afford to let the bears keep feeding on our beef."

I watched his face when he was telling me this and I could see the telltale worry line showing on his forehead. Not knowing, of course, that this time of year was the bear's most active feeding season.

Our main courses arrived along with more margaritas.

Over the course of our dinner, I asked more questions and the conversation continued.

"Tell me more about the ranch. Is it only cattle?"

"It's mainly cattle but we have horses too. And we grow lots and lots of hay. I have some new ideas about ranching, but my father is set in the old ways. But one day the ranch will be mine."

He had told me last night that he too was an only child. *Something we had in common.*

"There's something about the smell of fresh-cut hay. Or a new saddle. And the clean, crisp air on a fall morning," he shared with me.

It was obvious that he loved Montana by the way he described the vast, open areas with rolling hills and the mountains looming in the far distance.

But then, with a wink, he tried to impress me with his travels throughout Montana.

"The mountains divide the state into two distinct parts," he told me. "The eastern part, where I live, is mostly ranching and hay farming."

He described the weather: warmer and less snow in the eastern area and colder and more snow in the mountains.

"I've been to western Montana many times but there's not much ranching there. Lumber is big, as is rock mining. But recently, catering to rich tourists skiing down the mountain passes is where the money is," he stated, sounding bitter.

How interesting that each way of life evolved from the weather.

I got the impression that Jackson was trying to convince me that Montana was the best, most beautiful, most scenic, most wonderful place to ever live.

But then the tables were turned and Jackson started asking *me* questions.

"I've lived in the Midwest my entire life. Born and raised in Chicago and moved out here to the cornfields for college," I told him when he asked if I'd ever lived out of this area.

"Tell me about your mother?" he prodded.

"She died about a year ago. But we were very close."

I couldn't say much more without getting weepy. And I wasn't ready to share the *lack* of information about my father. If Jackson asked, I would just tell him what I tell most people when they ask—that he died before I was born.

I kept my answers as short as possible and my mouth full of food. I noticed he didn't act surprised that my mother was dead. And, curiously, he didn't ask about my father. Did he already know somehow? Had Lucy told him at the bar? I couldn't hear their entire conversation, but surely she would have told me if he was asking questions about me.

He didn't mind filling the gaps of silence and strangely didn't push me for more information on my family. But he did bring up my major.

"Why Literature?" he wondered out loud.

"Why not?" I countered. That sounded defensive, so I continued. "I've always loved to read. Books can take you anywhere. Michener's *Hawaii*. Pasternak's *Doctor Zhivago*. M. M. Kaye's *Shadow of the Moon*. Karen Blixen's *Out of Africa*. I've been to Hawaii, Russia, India, and Africa without ever leaving my apartment. I'd love to be able to instill that same enjoyment in young people. Reading is a hobby, if you will, that you can take with you anywhere."

He didn't seem familiar with any of those books, but I imagined he could hear the passion in my voice as I described my dream.

"Will you teach when you graduate?" he asked.

"I'm not sure. I might need an advanced degree," I explained.

"So have you applied to any graduate schools?"

"Not yet. I'm really not sure what I'll be doing a year from now," I confessed.

Finally, the waitress asked if we wanted anything else and he said, "No, just the check."

Now what? After just one dinner, I still wasn't ready to jump into bed with him. I anticipated that might be his plan, but he totally surprised me, yet again, by telling me he was going back to Montana the next day. He said he'd like to see me again when he came back.

"And when would that be?" I asked.

"Oh, hard to tell, but probably in a few weeks," he replied.

Something in the back of my brain said I should ask what exactly he was doing here with his uncle. But the opportunity to do so came and went.

"But in the meantime, give me your phone number. I'll call you from Montana to talk with you, darlin'."

~~~~~~

On the way back to his uncle's place, Jack was sure he had set the hook. He chuckled to himself—JT would love that fishing analogy. He kept asking about the *little filly out east* and Jack cringed every time. He didn't think Beth would cozy to being called a horse, no matter how good-looking the horse was. He could just hear her challenging his father on the comparison. Her sadness over her mom was obvious and she didn't volunteer any information about her father. Of course, he knew pretty much all of her history, but heck, he could play the game. And her not having any plans for a year from now worked perfectly for Jack's intentions.

~~~~~~

I settled back into my classes-swimming-studying-Friday-night-partying routine, and the next couple of weeks went by quickly. Jackson did as he promised and called regularly—

several times a week and, interestingly, often on Saturday mornings. I wondered if he was thinking about Lucy's after-the-bars parties and if I had slept alone. Not that it was any of his business, but of course I had. There was something about Jackson that was becoming quite attractive to me. I tried to convince myself that I was immune to his rugged good looks. I wasn't sure if it was his sexy drawl on the phone or his teasing sense of humor or the way he seemed truly interested in how my classes were going, but I began to look forward to his phone calls. I was *almost*—but not quite—so bold as to ask if he had made plans to visit his uncle again. I wasn't sure I wanted to encourage him. And if he did come back to visit, I wasn't sure how I could resist his charms.

Over the course of our many phone conversations, I learned that he was helping his Uncle Robert do some remodeling of his old house. There was a section of town, a few blocks over but still close to campus, that contained some big old mansions from back in the day. Many had been cannibalized into student housing, whether just rooms to rent or small apartments, but a few had been saved and, although run-down, were still recognizable from both the inside and the outside as fine old manors. One such belonged to Jackson's uncle, who was rehabbing it with help from Jackson and others. Jackson mentioned that his uncle taught at the university, but I kept forgetting to ask in what field. Jackson had a way of distracting me with entertaining stories of the ranch or his days at college, which were a great deal different than mine. He'd been a wild child on campus, according to his own admission.

I was curious to know if he had a girlfriend back in Montana. Or a couple of girlfriends. How was it that a guy as good-looking as Jackson was unattached?

I shyly broached the subject in one of our phone conversations. "Jackson, don't you have a girlfriend in Montana?"

"Beth, there aren't many women where I live," he told me.

Which didn't answer my question. "So, you came all the way to Illinois to hunt for one?" I teased.

In his sexiest drawl, he said, "And I'm sure glad I did, darlin'."

CHAPTER 3

On the day before Thanksgiving and the last day of classes before a long weekend, Jackson was sitting on the top step of my apartment building when I got home. Oddly, I was excited to see him again but asked why he didn't tell me he was coming.

"I wanted to surprise you, darlin'," he confessed. "And I never know if something at the ranch would cancel my plans at the last minute. Then I would disappoint you, sweetheart."

"How long are you staying?" I asked.

"I can stay 'til Sunday, darlin'. Can you put up with me that long?" he teased.

Stay where? I wondered to myself. Was he planning on staying in my apartment? In the same bed? My body betrayed me with a tingle *and a flutter. Damnit, was I falling under his spell? Was his charm simply irresistible?*

He took the bag of groceries from me while I unlocked the apartment. Luckily, I had done the dishes that morning. While I moved my textbooks and notebooks from the kitchen table, he started pulling groceries out of the bag. When he came to the sliced deli turkey, a box of stuffing mix, and a jar of gravy, he said, "Beth, is this your Thanksgiving dinner?"

What could I say? Yes, this was to be my poor man's holiday dinner.

"I'd planned to be all by myself, to work on a couple of papers that are coming due," I stammered. "Lucy went home," I mentioned, but didn't tell him that she was insistent that I come with her, until I finally lied and told her Jackson was coming. *Well, whew, not a liar after all.*

"Uncle Robert has given me instructions to invite you to his home for Thanksgiving dinner."

I raised an eyebrow.

Jackson's large hands fumbled into his jacket pocket and pulled out a slightly bent beige envelope. "Here, open it," he directed.

Doing so, I found not a formal invitation, but a handwritten note:

My dearest Elizabeth,

You are cordially invited to join us for Thanksgiving dinner, served when the turkey is done, sometime during one of the football games.

Robert Juddson

What a strange invite. His uncle obviously had a sense of humor.

"I'm not sure what time I should try to arrive, but I accept," I said, laughing. "What can I bring?"

"Nothing, darlin'. Just your pretty self and an appetite," he drawled.

Despite his assurance, I was brought up with the belief that if you're invited to someone's house for dinner, you don't show up empty-handed. My mother advised me to always keep a "nice"—meaning not cheap—bottle of wine just in case. *Thank you, Mom.*

Jackson's uncle's house was one of the largest old mansions on the historic block. He had invited several of his students and I could tell that undergrad and grad students alike respected him. It was fun watching Jackson and his uncle put the dinner together. They worked well together. The large dining room table was an exquisite antique and covered with any traditional Thanksgiving favorite imaginable. The conversation was lively, the food was wonderful, and the day went by quickly. We all watched football after the big meal. I snuggled next to Jackson and tried to impress him with my knowledge and understanding of the game.

"Once you grasp that each team gets *four* downs to get a *first* down, the rest is easy," I told him. "Although, I admit that I still don't get *all* the sexual references."

"What are you talking about, darlin'?" he asked indignantly, with a tone that said, "*How dare you sully the manly game of football?*"

"Well, forward *passes* and touch*downs*, not to mention *tight ends*. Sounds *sexy* to me," I replied innocently, emphasizing the innuendos. Maybe it was the wine at dinner or his damn sexiness so near to me that made me talk so boldly. I never talked like that, but I'd heard Lucy talk like this all the time. Not being much of a flirt, the color rose in my cheeks and I pointedly stared at the TV. Luckily, there were other conversations going on in the room and only Jackson had heard my comment.

He leaned close to me and whispered in my ear, "Darlin', I never thought of football *exactly* like that before, but I sure will from now on."

As I turned to see if he was serious or joking, he gently kissed me. It wasn't one of those hot and heavy, steam-up-the-windows kisses, but the gentle pressure of his lips on mine as well as his arm pulling me against him left no doubt about his feelings. I experienced a warm tingle in my belly that had nothing to do with all the food I'd eaten. And as gently as his kiss started, it ended much too quickly. But then I remembered we were sitting in a room full of people, watching a football game.

~~~~~~

Later that evening, everyone agreed they finally had room for some pumpkin pie. On my way back from the guest bathroom, I went to see if Jackson or his uncle needed any help. As I was about to enter the massive old kitchen, I overheard Jackson say, "She is so much prettier than that picture you gave me."

I couldn't hear what his uncle said, but it sounded like "I told you so."

What? Were they talking about me? And what picture?

Then I heard Jackson say, "Oh, there you are. Did you get lost?"

When I realized, he was talking to me, I stuttered, "No, no. Just wondered if I could help."

"Sure, darlin'. Wanna carry these plates and forks to the dining room?"

He handed over the stack of plates and forks and I headed to the dining room. I needed to talk to Lucy about what I had heard.

~~~~~~

Jackson drove me home during half-time of the late game. He walked me to my door but didn't come in. We made plans to meet the following afternoon, and after another very chaste kiss, he left. I hated to admit it, but I was looking forward to spending the long weekend with him.

On Friday, I showed him around campus, but most of the buildings were locked, except for the Student Union. We wandered around the Union, making our way to the lower-level "Tune Room," named for the free jukebox. There were only a handful of students sitting at the tables surrounding the dance floor.

For dinner, we helped ourselves to leftover turkey sandwiches at his uncle's. Later, we went back to the bar where we'd met. No band played, but their jukebox was blaring. To my surprise, Jackson led me onto the dance floor and impressed me with his moves, in spite of those boots.

Saturday, I needed to study and Jackson needed to help his uncle with the renovations. But we managed to sneak in a movie at the "previously released" bargain theater and shared a pizza at Rick's Pizza in the Pan. A local favorite. Voted best pizza year after year.

Just another chaste kiss when he dropped me off. But this time he was standing very close to me outside my apartment door, so there was a bit of body language happening between us. And I certainly could understand what his body was saying to mine. I think Lucy would be pleased to know he felt *large* through his blue jeans.

Sunday, we met for a late breakfast out before he had to leave for the airport. I had very mixed feelings about his departure. A part of me would miss him but another part of me wanted my safe, boring life back.

Lucy returned to campus late Sunday and came right over for a visit, bringing leftovers.

"You and Jackson have sex yet, Liz?" she boldly asked.

"Not that it's any of your business," I grinned, "but no, not yet."

"What is that man waiting for?" Lucy wondered. "How was the weekend otherwise?"

I told Lucy about the old mansion and Thanksgiving dinner. Then I told her what I thought I'd overheard.

"I can't be positive, but it sounded like he said, 'she's prettier than the picture you gave me.' What do you suppose *that* means? Do you think he's stalking me?"

"Why would he do that? He was at the bar and I invited him over," she mused. "It was a chance meeting." And then, excitedly, Lucy said, "Oh, Liz, remember that yearbook the university put out that *one* year? He and his uncle probably found your picture in that. Remember? That photographer snapped you coming out of class, carrying all those Lit books?" She laughed.

"Oh right, I had forgotten about that. I was in a hurry to get to the pool. Thank goodness he didn't photograph me in the pool." We both laughed. "You're probably right, Lucy. His uncle must have that yearbook and Jackson looked through it."

~~~~~~

On my own that evening, I couldn't help but think about Jackson. He was funny and so sexy. Maybe it was his size or maybe because he was older, but he came off as dependable. And strong. A man who could take care of his woman. That he'd given me only chaste kisses all weekend suggested he was trustworthy as well. He certainly wasn't pushing me toward the nearest mattress. I was beginning to feel quite comfortable with him. It was a bit scary, when I thought about it, because I'd never been this way with anyone else.

Whenever I was swimming, I could just pound the water and let my mind tackle my latest problems. *He lives on the other side of the country. How can any kind of relationship work with that distance? We have nothing in common. Why'd he choose me?*

But then I'd hear him say *darlin'* in that sexy voice and I'd look into those striking blue eyes, and all those thoughts would fade like the ripples I'd made swimming laps.

CHAPTER 4

When Jack got back to the ranch, although it was late, he wanted to see Cathy. As if by mental telepathy, there she appeared, riding up on her sorrel as he headed to the barn. It didn't take them long to find a dark corner and rediscover their passion for hot, quick sex.

She just had to cup his manhood through his jeans, and he was rock-hard. He stuck his hand down her pants, moved aside her panties, and shoved a finger, then two, into her. It didn't take much to get Cathy ready.

She shimmied out of her Levi's, turning them inside-out and shoving off her boots at the same time.

Jackson unzipped his fly, released his cock, and pushed Cathy up against the rough wall, spreading her legs with his thigh.

"I've missed you," she panted. "Fuck me, JJ."

Not needing any more encouragement, he plunged his cock into her.

It didn't last long for either of them. Out of breath, legs wobbling, they kissed a few times.

Cathy sighed. "I can't believe we can get so hot and so

high, after all these years." She sounded amazed.

Afterward, although Jack felt much better physically, he was struggling mentally, almost as if he'd been unfaithful to Beth. But he convinced himself that couldn't be true since he'd done nothing more than kiss her the entire weekend. But he wondered if she was as frustrated as he'd been. Before Cathy just took care of *that*.

"Are you tired, cowboy? You're kinda quiet tonight," Cathy asked as she struggled to turn her jeans right-side-out.

"Long day. Long flight. Yeah, I guess I am. I'd better get on in before JT sends Glenn out looking for me."

Cathy, jeans and boots back on, walked toward her horse.

"You'll be okay, riding back?" Jack asked her.

"Oh sure, JJ. You know me, eyes like a cat in the dark. And welcome home," she tossed back at him as she turned and blew him a kiss.

Jack watched Cathy effortlessly climb into the saddle and urge her mount into the night. Could he stop seeing her? If he married Beth, he'd have to, wouldn't he? Was this what he wanted? Would the sex be as hot with Beth as it was with Cathy?

His cock jerked just remembering his release moments ago in the barn. What if he told JT that Beth was not the least bit interested in him? What would JT do? *Make my life more miserable than it is now*, Jack supposed.

JT stood in the doorway as Jack made his way up the front steps. He braced himself for what was coming; he was pretty darn sure JT saw Cathy ride out of the yard.

"Sow your wild oats quickly, Jackson. But for godsakes don't get that slut pregnant," JT admonished.

Jack didn't engage, although his jaw clenched whenever he heard JT call Cathy that. He was too tired to pick a fight tonight. He walked around JT and headed inside.

~~~~~~

The days passed quickly on the ranch. There was always so much work to be done, and JT started riding Jack's ass the moment he got home.

"You have to get that herd moved before the snow gets too deep," he warned. "And there are some sick cattle that have to be tended."

"For fuck's sake, JT, doesn't anything get taken care of when I'm not here?" Jack loudly complained. "Where's Glenn? What's he been doing?"

"Don't you take that tone with me, Jackson!" JT shouted. "Glenn's a hired hand. Not the heir apparent."

Jack often wondered if Glenn was *more* than just a hired hand. Something about apples and trees, Jack had heard stories of JT's womanizing back in the day. And Glenn was treated differently than any other hired hand.

~~~~~~

The snow started falling a week after Thanksgiving and accumulated quickly with each new storm. Jack faithfully called Beth a couple of times a week, pouring on the charm. He couldn't remember ever working this hard to get a girl. But this wasn't just *any* girl, he reminded himself. As if he needed reminding. Seemed like his old man brought it up every day.

"When are you gonna marry that girl, Jackson?" JT asked once again at breakfast. "How long does it take you to woo her, for chrissakes?"

"Woo? JT, this is the seventies, not the forties. I'm working on it. It's not easy *wooing* her from a thousand miles away," Jack snipped.

In a rare moment of honesty, JT admitted, "Jack, I won't live forever. I'd like to see you married. And I'd like a grandson or two, so I'll know the ranch will carry on when I'm dirt-napping with your mother."

Jack didn't know how to reply to his father's confession, disgusted with JT's crudeness. But, just like every other moment, the guilt roiled when JT added, "And being stuck in this chair isn't helping my longevity."

Jack wanted to snap back that there were things JT could do—exercising and eating healthier—that might add some more birthdays. But Jack had too much work to do to waste his energy arguing with JT, knowing that whatever he or the doctor said wouldn't make a bit of difference.

CHAPTER 5

The last weeks before the end of the semester passed way too quickly for me. It was good to be busy with finals and end-of-semester projects. Those didn't leave me a lot of time to dwell on Jackson. He continued to call every few days and was charming as ever, but when I wasn't captivated by his intense gaze, my rational thoughts said this relationship would never work. *Montana is like a foreign country to me. I'm not sure how I feel about Jackson. He's not who I envisioned myself with. All dark and hairy and so big!* I swam as much as I could during finals week, but other than the chlorinated water, no solutions washed over me.

Lucy had left for home right after her last final, so not only was the town deserted, but the small apartment building was as well. The campus was quiet; not many students were still around since the semester had ended, and soon even the university buildings would be closed for their annual shutdown.

I've spent other holidays alone, I told myself. *I've managed before and I'll manage this time too.* I had already bought the textbooks for the next—my last!—semester, and I thought I'd get a head start on some of the reading. Maybe I'd drive into the city and visit a museum or the Art Institute.

Right before Lucy left, she asked me where I was with grad school applications.

"Liz, why don't you apply to grad school in Arizona? Come with me. We could get an apartment together."

"Lucy, what's the point in staying with Literature when I'll never get a teaching job?" I complained.

"Well, Liz, what *are* you going to do after graduation?"

"I'll send out some *more* résumés to some *more* local high schools, and hope for an opening," I promised her.

~~~~~~

Jackson hadn't mentioned coming back; perhaps he didn't want to get my hopes up. And the weather in Montana could not only delay but also entirely cancel his travel plans.

Then, the week before Christmas, Jackson called to say he was flying out in a few days. No surprise visit this time. He asked if I could pick him up at the airport. That surprised me a little, but I agreed. I did some fast Christmas shopping and made a batch of Christmas cookies, and a few days later, I left my apartment to go to the airport.

It was snowing lightly as I got on the tollway to O'Hare. Traffic was not heavy, and I had plenty of time. I drove past the "*Welcome to CHICAGO-O'HARE INTERNATIONAL AIRPORT, Richard J. Daley, Mayor*" banner and followed the signs to the short-term parking lot. Elevators and escalators later, I found Jackson's terminal. After checking the arrival/departure boards, I headed toward the gate to meet his flight. Then *more* waiting. Eventually, I saw the plane taxiing up to the jetway.

Several passengers got off ahead of Jackson. As if by instinct, we saw each other and *only* each other. His eyes locked onto mine and my heart sent a flutter to my brain. He was undeniably conspicuous with his height and those darn good looks. He gave me a brief kiss and a one-armed hug, which was more like a squeeze since he was carrying his duffel bag over his other arm. No need to go to baggage claim, he told me. *He packed remarkably light. How do men do that?*

As we headed to the parking garage, he said, "Darlin', I'll drive. Give me the keys."

I started to protest. He didn't ask; he just *told* me. If any kind of warning bell dinged, I ignored it. Besides, it *was* still snowing, and if he drove, I could just *look* at him on the way back, so I dug around in my purse for the keys and handed them over.

Snow had accumulated on both windshields while I'd been in the terminal.

"Where's your scraper, Beth?"

"There, behind the driver's seat," I pointed out.

It was one of those combination ice scraper and snow brushes, but mine was only a brush, as the scraper end had busted off last winter.

He picked it up and rolled his eyes. "What do you do if you have to scrape ice off the windshield?" he asked.

"I turn the defrost on high and listen to the radio," I said demurely.

~~~~~~

After we got back to my apartment, stomped the snow off our boots, and removed our winter coats, Jackson took my arm and pulled me to him.

"Let me give you a proper hug," he growled as he wrapped those strong arms around me. Pressing me up against his body, he lowered his head for a kiss. This time, it wasn't chaste. Far from it.

He kissed me gently at first, but possessively pressed

my body to his. He tasted, then sampled more, and finally devoured. My pulse quickened and my tummy tumbled and other parts, lower down, tingled. My goodness, this man could kiss. I briefly wondered how he had gotten so adept, but the thought left just as quickly as his kiss deepened and his tongue parted my lips for further plundering.

Of course, I had been kissed before. But never like this. I was encompassed, surrounded by his strength. This was so intense. I grabbed a fistful of his shirt to hang on, and kissed him back. This kiss had desire, but also hope and promise and trust. It was getting obvious that Jackson was turned on. I was too, but I wasn't totally sure I was ready for that ultimate step—or fall, more like.

Jackson seemed to sense my feelings, or I hoped that was what happened, as he released first my lips and then the rest of me. I wasn't sure I could stand on my own, but somehow, I didn't collapse in a tangle at his feet. *How embarrassing that would have been.*

Grabbing a couple of beers and heading for my living room couch, he told me that his uncle always traveled over the holidays. Many professors did. Several I knew from my classes had already taken off for exotic, warmer places under the guise of *research*.

"Beth, he asked that I watch over his house while he's gone," he informed me. "He hates to ask any of his students to bring in his mail and water the plants. So, we'll have chores," he added with a wink.

And there was that flutter, down low in my tummy. That wink certainly did not have anything to do with collecting mail or watering plants.

~~~~~~

Jackson took me out to dinner that evening. He found many excuses to touch me: gripping my arm as we walked across an icy spot in the parking lot; his hand on the small of my back once inside, guiding me to our table; wrapping his hand over mine several times at dinner. And he told me how much he had missed me.

"Beth, these weeks since Thanksgiving have dragged. I could hardly wait 'til I could see you again," he admitted.

I was completely captivated.

After dinner, he had me drop him at his uncle's house.

Probably best to let both of us cool off a bit.

~~~~~~

Jack really didn't want to cool off. He knew he shouldn't rush Beth. Didn't want to spook her and have her shy away. Damn his father. Now *he* was using horse analogies. But Jack was eager to move forward. What he didn't tell Beth was that he and his uncle had schemed up this "house-sitting" plan a few weeks ago. And if by *woo* JT meant *seduce*, then that was Jack's plan for Christmas.

Uncle Robert had taken Jack to the pool gallery several times, where, unobserved by Beth, he could not only study her swimming strokes but also her swimsuit-clad body. He was thinking it would be a nice Christmas present to have Beth wrap those long legs of hers around him while he rode her. She had certainly responded to his kiss earlier. There was hope that sex with her wouldn't just be a husbandly duty. He was startled when he realized he was thinking of Beth, not Cathy.

~~~~~~

The next day, Jackson and I went to an afternoon movie. We saw the re-release of *Kelly's Heroes*. Well, *saw* isn't quite accurate. We *listened* to the movie. The theater was not crowded. We sat way in the back and, like a couple of high school kids, we necked through the entire movie. At one point, Jackson put his hand under all my winter layers and was rewarded with a naked breast. When his thumb played over my erect nipple, his breathing hitched, but mine stopped. It was so damn sexy. And exciting. I almost wished we were not at the movies but someplace closer to a bed. Or at least a *clean* floor.

After the movie, we went to one of the bars that served food. Nothing fancy, just burgers and beers. It was a place where the "townies" went to eat. But the savvy student knew about the great sandwiches and cheap beer.

"What should we do tomorrow, darlin'?" The look in his eyes told me what he would like to do.

"Jackson, I was thinking that I'd like to cook dinner for you."

When I suggested a home-cooked meal, his eyes took on a funny sparkle, but he said, "Only if it's not too much work for you, Beth."

"I love to cook," I stated. *I might also love to cook for you.* "I need some time to grocery shop," I told him. But what I really needed was some time to myself to think. I was tumbling toward that fall, and I had to decide: was that what I really wanted, or was it just his overpowering charisma pushing me there?

He admitted there were some things he needed to take care of for his uncle, so we agreed he would come by around five o'clock the next day.

I thought long and hard about what to make. And about another *thing* possibly long and definitely hard. I finally came up with an Italian dinner. I was determined not to make *meat and potatoes*, which I imagined was the cowboy's standard. A nice Italian salad, garlic bread, and a mostaccioli-type casserole with pasta sauce, sausage, and mushrooms. *Does he even like mushrooms?*

The casserole was my one concession to any cowboy ways.

Red wine instead of beer. I had one "good" bottle left in my supply. And I would make tiramisu, using my mother's recipe. It required effort and careful attention, but I thought it would top off the meal.

I shopped early the next morning for the ingredients. I did as much of the preparations during the day as I could so everything would be mostly ready for the evening, all the while thinking about what might come next in this relationship.

Jackson called midafternoon and asked what he could bring.

"Just an appetite, Jackson." *And your sexy self.*

I got a long, silent pause in response and wasn't sure if he thought I meant appetite for food or for something else.

~~~~~~

Jackson arrived a few minutes early, with another bottle of red wine. Judging by the label, I thought his bottle might be from a higher shelf in the liquor department.

"Beth, it smells amazing. Italian?" he guessed.

"Yes. I hope you like mushrooms."

"There are few things I won't eat, Beth," he said with a wink. "What can I do to help? How about I open the wine?"

Again, he didn't wait for an answer. This was definitely part of his character. *Is this something I can tolerate?* I wondered.

"The main course is not quite done. Yes, Jackson, some wine while I finish making the salad would be nice," I conceded. I didn't want our first home-cooked dinner to get off to a bad start.

He reached around me to look in my cabinets for wine glasses. On the third try, he found them and took two down. Then he rummaged around until he found a corkscrew.

Make yourself at home, I thought.

"Do you like red?" he asked, albeit a bit late, since he already had the bottle open.

"Yes, with food and in moderation. Too much can give me a headache. I'm really not much of a drinker," I admitted.

"You're not much of a pot smoker either, Beth," he pointed out.

Feeling defensive, I said, "I don't particularly enjoy marijuana, no. Messes with my head. But I take a toke now and again to be polite."

Leaning toward me, he said in a low voice, "Well, Beth, we'll just have to find something you *do* enjoy."

The suggestion was evident. The hint was unmistakable. I went to crack open the kitchen window, despite the chilly weather outside. The kitchen's warmth intensified, and it wasn't solely due to the oven's heat.

Moving away, I started to whisk the homemade salad dressing, a simple mix of oil, vinegar, and spices that I tossed over the lettuce, black olives, and peppers. As I picked up the large bowl to carry it to the table, Jackson said, "Wait, I'll get that."

The oven timer dinged just then, and I slid the casserole dish onto a large cutting board on the counter. "My table is too small for everything, so grab your plate and help yourself to some 'mostaccioli bake.' One of my mother's concoctions," I told him, pointing to the small wooden recipe box on a nearby shelf.

Setting both glasses of wine on the table, he carried his plate over to the counter. "Beth, it smells amazing and looks delicious. Here, let me scoop some for you."

And with that, he gave me a cowboy-sized serving, which I'd never be able to finish.

~~~~~~

Over dinner, we quizzed each other about past Christmas holidays and our favorite traditions. We found we had quite a bit in common: we both loved big Christmas trees with a lot of passed-down ornaments and tinsel, never garland. And we completely agreed: snow was a must for Christmas.

"Carols shouldn't start until December eleventh," I insisted. "Any earlier, and you'll be sick of 'Rudolph' and 'Silent Night' by the twenty-fifth," I added, laughing.

"Food?" he asked.

"It doesn't have to be turkey again, but that is a must for Thanksgiving," I told him.

"How do you feel about venison, Beth?"

I don't think I could eat Bambi. "I've never had it," I admitted. "Cookies?" I had to know, because I loved to bake.

"Yes."

"Eggnog?"

"Definitely. But it must be spiked." He winked.

~~~~~~

It was obvious Jackson enjoyed the dinner, not only because he told me several times, but also because he had to stop himself from having a third helping. He helped me clear the table and I started some sudsy water to soak the dinner dishes. He stepped behind and started to hug me, but with the water running I didn't realize he was that close. Startled and with a squeal, I turned the sink sprayer on him and sprinkled him. Just a quick spray.

I watched for his reaction. Would he be upset? Would he get even, grab the sprayer, and soak me?

He just laughed, shook his head, and said, "Well, I didn't expect that. Remind me not to sneak up on you. Glad that was only a sink sprayer and not a frying pan," he joked.

Leaving the dishes to soak, we took what was left of the

second bottle of wine and pieces of tiramisu into the living room and settled on the couch in front of my Christmas tree.

We continued our discussion of holiday customs. We both loved real trees.

Lucy had helped me manhandle my small tree in through the front door. We'd made some eggnog and started decorating it, first with a string of colorful blinking lights, then my mom's old ornaments and a few others I had collected on my own. It still looked a little bare, so we had made some popcorn, which we mostly ate, and strung a bag of cranberries as well, which, truthfully, were a lot easier to string than popcorn.

"I string popcorn and cranberries for my tree every year," I told Jackson. "Afterwards, I remove the ornaments and lights, and put the tree in the yard. I leave the cranberries and popcorn for the birds to enjoy."

However, we vehemently disagreed on opening presents.

"When I got older, my mom and I started opening presents on Christmas Eve. Then we could sleep in on Christmas Day," I told him.

"Presents should only be opened on the morning of Christmas Day," Jackson argued.

We both got quiet, lost in our own thoughts. Neither of us wanted to ruin the glow, so the topic of opening presents was dropped.

I snuggled close to Jackson, and between the wine, the Italian food, and the dim lighting cast only by the lights on the tree, I got sleepy.

"Beth," he said softly.

As I turned toward him, he gently kissed me. Deepening the kiss, I realized I wasn't sure I wanted to go further tonight. I'd had a lot of wine. But my traitorous body betrayed me.

I kissed him back, grabbed a handful of that dark hair, and gently tugged, trying to bring him closer. If that was even possible.

"I think it's time I headed to my uncle's," Jackson said, almost questioningly.

"Mmm, all right. I guess. Probably best. I'm sure I've had too much wine." I knew I was stammering.

"Take two aspirin with a large glass of water before you go to sleep," he advised.

Earlier, he had insisted we spend the following night, Christmas Eve, at his uncle's house. When I mumbled something about my apartment, he pointed out that his uncle's house was much larger *and* it had a fireplace.

~~~~~~

On the way back to his uncle's, Jack once again congratulated himself. Beth was a great cook. Damn. He had gotten so lucky. He was impressed with the wonderful Italian dinner: the food was delicious, and everything was ready at the same time, which she made happen so effortlessly. There weren't piles of dirty pots and pans in the sink or on the counters. The only time Cathy had ever cooked for him, the kitchen was a disaster. Tonight, everything was perfect. Especially that tiramisu. Beth was not only pretty *and* sexy, but she was also smart. And she had a playful side. That surprised him—she could be so shy. He couldn't wait to see how all of her personality meshed sexually. He probably could have had her tonight, but he knew that she'd had too much wine, and that wasn't how he wanted her for the first time. He could wait another day. Tomorrow night, he would find out. He had it all planned. His cock twitched in anticipation.

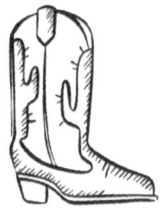

CHAPTER 6

Jackson picked me up around noon and said it was his turn to cook dinner for me. It was snowing again, with measurable accumulation predicted, so he suggested that I stay over.

"There are plenty of bedrooms in the big old house," he assured me.

I had a feeling that tonight might be The Night. And really, having our *first time* on Christmas Eve *would* be pretty romantic.

After our days together at Thanksgiving, I had sensed that *it* was going to happen sooner rather than later. Jackson was taking it slow, but he also didn't impress me as someone who embraced celibacy in a relationship. So, with Lucy's urging and companionship, I went to the University Clinic for some birth control pills. After a brief, embarrassing exam and a few questions about my cycles, I was good to go, so to speak. I was advised that the pill was only about ninety-three percent effective, but I wasn't sure I really needed birth control pills as years ago, during my first pelvic exam, I was told I had a "tipped uterus" and it might be difficult, if not impossible, to get pregnant. When I had shared this news with my mom, we both cried and hugged. I had never tested that theory as I was hopeful that the doctor was wrong or that getting pregnant would only be *difficult* rather than *impossible*. But I thought it was too early in this relationship to share all that with Jackson.

I brought the leftover tiramisu. Hopefully, it would complement whatever Jackson was making for dinner. *I hope it's not venison.* I carried a large purse with a change of underwear, my toothbrush, and the birth control pills.

I was nervous, but Jackson had a calming effect. He handed me a beer as we started a tour of the house. I had seen parts of it at Thanksgiving but only on the main level. There were three floors, the top being attic-like with slanted ceilings and odd-shaped rooms. At the very bottom, there was an old, creepy basement with a monstrous, rackety furnace and a darker corner with a dirt floor.

Jackson pointed out the renovations that had been completed. Most of the main level was finished. Upstairs, only three of the five bedrooms had been updated and just two of the three bathrooms were functional. The attic area needed the most work, as did the basement. But Jackson's uncle was doing the renovations slowly and tastefully, all while trying to keep as much of the original woodwork and plaster moldings as possible.

The main level of the house was beautifully decorated for Christmas. Boughs of evergreen garland tied with large red bows wound around the stair banisters. A huge old-fashioned Christmas tree, trimmed with what looked like a hundred ornaments, candy canes, tastefully draped tinsel, and soft white lights, dominated the living room. Much more impressive than my small tree with a few hand-me-down ornaments. I could see why Jackson wanted to spend Christmas here. To the left of the tree, there was a massive fireplace with an ornately carved wood mantel from which stockings hung, just like in any classic Christmas movie.

Jackson apparently had laid some firewood in the grate earlier and now he bent down and lit it. Standing, he took my beer from my hand and set it on an end table, then pulled me toward him into a tight hug. He tipped my chin up and moved his head closer to kiss me. Dear me, that man could kiss. Being pressed up against him and held so tightly, I understood how Scarlett could tell Rhett she might faint. We came up for air, and he maneuvered me to the sofa. The kissing resumed, along with some caressing. My sweater came off, as did his. The fire in the fireplace was heating up, as were we. Eventually, I was in a near-prone position on the couch with Jackson wedged against me. His hand had been under my shirt and was now moving south to the outside of my jeans. I pressed against him, silently urging him: *Yes! Touch me down there.*

"Beth," he said, "Are you comfortable?"

What? What a strange question to ask me right now.

"Honestly," I said, "I'm afraid you're going to fall off the couch."

With minimum movement, he started tossing cushions and blankets off the back of the couch onto the floor in front of the sofa. Then he rolled, taking me with him—*on top of him*—to the makeshift mattress.

Well, that was a slick move, I thought as I resettled against him. But quick enough, most thought was again wiped out by his incredible kissing.

I was melting, blood was pooling in my lady parts, my panties were damp, and Jackson was hard. *Oh my, this was happening.* My jeans came off, and then his. He was really adept at getting my clothes off. I was left in my T-shirt and panties.

"Darlin', am I gonna need a condom?" he asked.

I'm sure I blushed scarlet. "No...no," I stammered. "I'm on the pill."

And with that, the rest of my clothes were off and Jackson

was seriously exploring, fondling, kissing me all over... It was sensory overload! When he slipped his finger inside of me, I arched my back and made a humming noise. This obviously turned Jackson on as I could feel his penis twitch against my thigh. And it was large. *Will IT fit?* was about the only conscious thought I had.

He continued to finger me, adding a second finger, which I greedily accepted. I was very wet. He ditched his drawers and got on top. But he went so very slowly, just easing a bit of that big bad boy inside me gently, a little at a time. He would pull out now and again, and then start all over. I was afraid at one point that I was going to have to *beg* him to get it ALL *in there*. But when he was finally all inside me, my insides quivered with the most intense pleasure ever.

"That's it, darlin', just give it up." He pushed a few more times and I felt him shake and heard him moan.

Wow, so that's what an orgasm feels like. It was my first!

Way too soon, Jackson withdrew and snuggled next to me, pulling blankets over us both.

"Are you okay, Beth?"

"Mmmmm..." I was still relishing the glow of My First.

"Want another beer?"

"Mmnnn..." I hummed in a negative tone.

"Hungry?"

"Mmmm..." I murmured in a *maybe* pitch.

He just chuckled and wrapped those strong arms around me. He was quiet for quite a while, and I wondered if he was asleep. Lucy told me that falling asleep afterward often happened with men. Then he softly asked me if I was sore. Thank goodness, he couldn't see my face in the winter shadows and low firelight. His question made me flush with a rosy glow that had nothing to do with what had happened a few minutes ago.

"Um, maybe a little, but it was worth it. I feel good," I

purred, stretching next to him.

"You do?" He sounded—what? Pleased?

"Mmmm, yes, that was so intense." I added, without much thought, "I've never felt anything like that before."

Jackson got quiet again, and I was hoping he *was* asleep this time so I didn't have to answer any more questions.

Eventually, though, he had to move to put more wood on the fire.

"Beth, I need to start dinner," he told me.

Drowsily, I said, "Okay." But *I* didn't move much.

I was rewarded with a nice long look at his naked backside as he first reclaimed, then shinnied into his underwear. He stoked the fire and then added a few more logs. Leaving the room, he returned shortly with two foil-wrapped lumps and a pair of long tongs.

"What are those?"

"The potatoes." He nestled them into the embers in the fireplace.

Oh boy—oh *cowboy*. Cooking in the fireplace.

He said he would grill some steaks in an hour or so. I just couldn't help it—I snickered out loud. Covering the noise with a little cough, as I didn't want to hurt his feelings or insult his Montana manliness, I thought to myself, *Yep, meat and potatoes*.

But in his defense, he had prepared a wonderful salad, with a homemade dressing. And the leftover tiramisu rounded out a delicious meal.

After dinner and another beer, when the fire was down to glowing wood embers, he nudged my sleepy body and suggested we go upstairs to one of the beds.

His lovemaking was even more fabulous the second time. Out-of-this-world wonderful. He would bring me almost to the brink and have me just about to beg, then would slow the pace. By the time he finally entered me, I was ready, wet, and very willing. And miracles of miracles, that intense, almost unbearable pleasure overtook me. Two for two. The man was amazing. And with that thought, I fell asleep tangled up in the sheets and Jackson.

~~~~~~

Jack stayed awake a while longer, holding Beth gently. She'd never had an orgasm? He was stunned that he had given her the first one. *And* the second. He smiled to himself. That made him feel...what? Proud, of course, but also protective of her. He'd never felt this way about Cathy, or any of the other women before Cathy. With those women, it was mutually satisfying, but they usually tried a little harder to please *him* than the other way around.

Beth had been special to him because of *who* she was, but now she was *extra* special to him in a *very* intimate connection. And she was *his*. Maybe he didn't have a ring on her finger or a marriage certificate with her name on it, but she now *belonged* to him. She wasn't a virgin, he could tell, but her experiences must have been so limited as to never have enjoyed an orgasm. This was almost...no, it *was* better than taking her virginity. The boys she'd been with must have been too wrapped up in their own pleasure to care about hers. *Bastards*, he thought angrily. He held Beth a bit tighter and closer and drifted off to sleep as well.

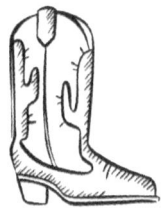

CHAPTER 7

I awoke in the morning to the smell of bacon. After using my toothbrush and having a quick wash, I attempted to do something with my thoroughly tousled hair. I looked for a brush on top of the chest of drawers and in the adjoining bathroom, but either Jackson didn't have one or it was tucked away somewhere else. Glancing at myself in the bathroom mirror, I was now determined to find a brush.

I snooped further, peering *into* the drawers of the large chest. The very top drawer held keys, his wallet, and, *voila*, a brush. When I picked it up, a half-sheet of loosely folded paper popped up from under the hairbrush. I hadn't meant to look at it, but something about the size and color of the paper looked familiar. Opening it, I was shocked to see that it was a copy of my fall class schedule. Courses, times, buildings, room numbers; all the information anyone would need to know where I was at any given time. *Why on earth would he have my schedule?* Not wanting to get caught rummaging through his dresser, I put the schedule back as I found it. I quickly ran the brush through my hair and replaced it on top of the paper.

Hastily fashioning my hair into a long, loose braid, I headed downstairs.

How could I confront Jackson without admitting I was snooping? I needed a chance to figure out how, and when, he came to have a printed copy of my schedule. *I needed to talk to Lucy.*

Walking into the kitchen, I saw Jackson standing at the stove, looking damn sexy. He was dressed casually in a T-shirt, jeans, and slippers but no socks. My mouth watered but I'm pretty sure it was from the plate piled high with bacon. Mostly, anyway.

"Sit down," he encouraged. "Eggs are just about done."

Next to the bacon, he placed a basket of biscuits on the table. In answer to the surprised look on my face, Jackson explained, "Every cowboy worth his beans can make biscuits, darlin'. The trick is keeping them light and moist, not doughy. But cooked through. I do admit that cooking biscuits on a campfire can be a challenge."

"Did you make these in the fireplace, like the potatoes?" I teased him.

"No," he chuckled, "I used the oven."

But I couldn't imagine cooking *anything* on a campfire, let alone biscuits.

Bringing two plates with eggs to the table, he sat down. "Dig in," he instructed.

Once I smelled the food, I was surprised at how hungry I was.

"These biscuits are amazing," I complimented him. "And the bacon is crisp, just the way I like it."

Golly gee, the man could cook. And kiss. And, of course, *other* things.

~~~~~~

After helping Jackson clean up the kitchen from breakfast, we each took one more cup of coffee out to the loveseat in front of the Christmas tree.

"Beth, do you think that since we *know* each other now, you could call me Jack? My father is the only one who calls me Jackson," he said with a frown.

There was something in his look, and his tone, left unsaid about his father, but I didn't push. And yes, now that we've been *intimate*, calling him "Jack" did seem more friendly. *Should I tell him that he is the only one who calls me Beth?* I had to admit the shortened name was growing on me and Elizabeth did sound too formal after last night.

"Do you have to think on it that long?" he asked.

"Merry Christmas, Jack," I said to him.

"Merry Christmas, Beth," he whispered, his beard tickling my neck.

Oh, Christmas—I had almost forgotten.

"I have a present for you, Jack."

I retrieved a package from behind some other boxes under the tree. He looked surprised as I handed it to him. I was pleased because I was pretty sure he had been busy in the kitchen when I slipped his present from my big purse to its hiding place under the tree.

Then it was my turn to be surprised. Last evening, in the low light, I didn't notice that one of the traditional stockings had my name on it. He unhooked it from the mantel and handed it to me. Nestled in amongst the dozen candy kisses, there was an ice scraper for my car windows.

"How thoughtful," I said, smiling.

"There's more," he said, encouraging me to take another look.

At the bottom of the stocking was a small box. My heart beat so loud, I was sure he could sense it. I picked it up to shake it, but I wasn't sure I wanted to open this tiny present. *Surely, it wouldn't be a ring, would it?* It was way too soon and we hardly knew each other.

Carefully unwrapping the Christmas paper, I discovered the small box held a beautiful gold chain carrying a miniature gold horseshoe. I was relieved rather than disappointed. The necklace was truly beautiful and unique. Upon closer examination, I noticed two tiny sparkly chips, one on each open end of the charm.

"They're lucky, you know, *darlin'*." In response to my puzzled look, he added, "Horseshoes. And you always display a horseshoe in the 'U' position so the luck doesn't fall out." And then he winked at me, so I wasn't sure if that last part was true or something he just made up.

"Will you help me put it on?" I asked, pulling my braid out of the way.

I worried about those big hands working the clasp, but he had no trouble at all. Placing a light kiss on my bare neck, he whispered, "There you go, Beth."

I fingered the horseshoe, hanging at the perfect length. "It's beautiful, and so unique," I told him. "Thank you, Jack." I bent forward to give him a kiss. "Now open mine," I insisted.

My present to him was sort of a joke. It was an 8-track tape of Conway Twitty's album *Hello Darlin'*. I knew he liked country music but I didn't know much about it. I had laughed out loud in the store when I saw the album title.

After he tore the paper off his present, he had a twinkle in his eyes and a smile hiding in his beard. "Why thank you, *darlin'*," he heavily drawled. "There's one more present, Beth, but it's upstairs," he said, pulling me off the loveseat.

I let him lead me up the stairs, but when we walked past the bed, I asked him where we were going.

"Allow me a fantasy, would you, Beth?" he teased.

He gently pushed me into the bathroom and started peeling off my clothes in a practiced manner. He quickly slipped out of his jeans and T-shirt. Turning the water on in the shower, he moved aside the curtain and said, "Step in, darlin'."

It might have been *his* fantasy, but it was another *first* for me. Getting soapy and slippery in the shower led to activities *in addition* to getting clean. And to use Lucy's words, he once again rocked my world.

~~~~~~

Jack stayed for two entire weeks. And we spent those days however we wished. Making love in the morning or in the afternoon, but especially in the evenings in front of the fireplace. One night, after a particularly passionate coupling, we just slept there in front of the fireplace, too satiated to get up off the floor, snuggled in a huge pile of blankets.

Another day, when we were in the shower, all soapy and slippery again, he said, "I wonder if I suds you all up if I could slip you into my duffel and bring you back on the plane with me?"

I didn't say anything, but I'm sure I had a funny look on my face. We had not talked in any way about The Future.

"But you'd have to be real quiet like, darlin', and I doubt you could do that." And demonstrating his point, he slipped his hand under my butt cheek and squeezed. Proving him correct, I yelped!

~~~~~~

We spent most of the time at his uncle's house, stopping by my apartment from time to time to collect my mail and Lucy's and to pick up clean clothes. We cooked and we ate leftovers. We talked and we napped on the couch together. We watched a horror movie one night, and during the scary scenes I would bury my face in his shirt. We hiked in the snow all over the deserted campus. We watched the local kids skating on the pond.

One day, we took the train into Chicago and visited the Science and Industry Museum. Jack was quite interested in the two most popular exhibits: the coal mine and the submarine.

When I didn't show the same enthusiasm, I had to confess that I'd seen both, many times.

"Every year past fourth grade, this museum was a class trip. We'd spend the morning here and the afternoon at Adler Planetarium. A rite of passage for Chicago school kids."

I suggested the Shedd Aquarium instead of the planetarium for our afternoon. If I'd been by myself, or even with Lucy, I would have spent the afternoon at the Art Institute. I just wasn't sure Jack would enjoy that as much as seeing the fish.

We dashed into Marshall Fields, just so I could show him their famous forty-foot Christmas tree. Then we had burgers and beers at the Billy Goat Tavern before catching the last express train back to the cornfields.

Another day, we went to the movies to see John Wayne in *Big Jake*. It didn't surprise me one bit that Jack was a huge John Wayne fan.

"The Duke has a new movie coming out—*The Cowboys*," he stated. "I hope I can break away from the ranch to see it."

But we did not agree on New Year's Eve plans. I suggested we hit the bars. I thought it would be fun, celebrating with Jack.

"It's amateur night, darlin'. And it's snowing. Best to stay in and be safe."

I was surprised by this and thought about arguing, but before I could launch my initial defense, he swept me into those strong arms and started kissing me. When he let me go, I'd forgotten any idea about going out. So, New Year's Eve was quietly spent at his uncle's instead of the noisy bar. Another first for me.

Jack made it special with some chilled champagne and we

made love at midnight.

"What a wonderful way to start a new year," I declared.

~~~~~~

Eventually, the day came when he had to go back to Montana. Since Uncle Robert was still traveling, I had to take him to the airport. Saying goodbye would be tough. I'd gotten so used to being with him. Days *and* nights. As he drove to the airport, I fingered my horseshoe charm and tried to decide if I should tell him how I felt; how much I would miss him. My mother had warned me years ago that men don't want to hear a lot of mush. I thought it best to wait and take his lead on the goodbyes.

It started to snow again before we even got to the airport. Jack announced, "I'm just going to pull up and hop out. I want you to turn right around and head back before the weather gets any worse. I don't want to worry about you on the road, and Beth, I don't want any arguments."

This last part must have been in response to the look on my face.

Wow. Any *mushy* thoughts I might have had evaporated. He could be so bossy. I knew he was only concerned about my safety, and I *liked* that about him, but there would not be much time for any declarations of love or, at the very least, tender sentiments.

Not much more was said the rest of the way to O'Hare. He pulled up to the curb by departures and hopped out, as did I. As I came around to get in the driver's side, he pulled me in for a hug and said, "I'm gonna miss you, darlin'. Be good. I'll call you later to let you know I got home." He delivered a brief but meaningful kiss and walked toward the terminal.

On the drive back, I struggled with the parting. I alternated between being miffed that there weren't *more* words and then impressed that he cared so much about my safety. I didn't know what I was expecting. A declaration of love? A promise of undying devotion?

Jack's departure happened so fast. Damn the weather. But his protective concern for my drive back to the cornfields was a demonstration of how he would take care of a woman.

~~~~~~

Lucy returned to campus a few days after Jack left. After tossing her bags into her apartment, she immediately came over. She only had to take one look at me.

"Finally! So, how was it?" she demanded.

"Oh please, how can you tell? Is it that obvious?" I countered.

"Yep. You're glowing and you're dewy-eyed," she laughed.

"My eyes are not *dewy*," I insisted.

"So, tell. Can that cowboy ride or what, Liz?"

"Oh, stop, Lucy. It was actually pretty romantic. Christmas Eve, in front of the fireplace," I confided. "And we spent two whole weeks together. We walked and talked. Went to a movie. I even took him to Chicago," I gushed. Then, not wanting to share any more details, I asked, "How was your holiday, Lucy?"

"We two had hayrides. One during the day with all the kids. And another in the evening, with hot buttered rum for the adults. Everyone went to midnight services on Christmas Eve. But the kids woke us all up at six a.m. My oldest sister is expecting. Again," she rattled off.

"That makes three, right?"

"Yep, that'll make me six times an aunt," she boasted. "Does Jack have any siblings? Maybe you'll be an aunt one day too." She chuckled.

"I think you're putting the hay wagon before the horse,

Lucy. Just because I slept with him doesn't mean I'll marry him," I laughed.

After she left, I realized I had forgotten to get Lucy's thoughts on the copy of my class schedule being in Jack's dresser drawer.

CHAPTER 8

The next few weeks were really difficult. I truly missed Jack. I went through the motions of classes and swimming, but when I came back to the empty apartment, I didn't want to do much else. Jack would call, of course, but it wasn't the same. I couldn't *see* his face or *touch* him. I couldn't run my fingertips over the short hairs of his beard that were soft when stroked in a downward direction but were a tickly turn-on when he was nuzzling my thighs. I couldn't see the desire in those seductive blue eyes. And I could not see how this long-distance relationship would work.

At Lucy's urging, I sent out my résumé to local schools. I even mailed a grad school application to Lucy's school just to get her to quit pestering me.

When Jack didn't call for several days, I moped around the apartment, feeling moody and irritable. One Friday afternoon, Lucy came over to see if I wanted to go to the bars and I snapped at her. I apologized immediately but she laughed and said I just needed a good romp. Or a roll in a hayfield, she added teasingly. And yes, *that* was part of it, but I just missed his company.

My literature classes were a struggle. The Romantic Period course had sounded like fun—Brontë, Austen—but our first reading was Mary Wollstonecraft's *A Vindication of the Rights of Woman*. Written just shy of two hundred years ago, it proposed an interesting premise: women are not inherently inferior to men; they only *seem to be* because they lack education. An intriguing angle juxtaposed her writing on what was happening in the country at the time: women's lib, burn your bra, equal rights. Just walking on campus, it was obvious there were more men enrolled than women.

My other course, The English Novel Since 1900, didn't have an easy read either. *Finnegans Wake* by James Joyce. The only thing possibly worse would have been *Ulysses*.

I had a difficult time staying focused on my reading. My mind would drift to Christmas Eve in front of the fireplace. And soapy showers.

~~~~~

Once back in Montana, Jack quickly got wrapped up in winter ranching tasks. Although there was less work in the winter, the chores they did have to perform were much harder due to the cold and the snow. Trucks and tractors hesitated to start or wouldn't start at all. When you thought a truck was the correct vehicle for the day, you sometimes got it stuck in the snow and then needed the tractor to pull you out. Cattle and horses still had to be fed and watered. And besides checking fences, winter was the time all the ranch equipment was repaired, maintained, and readied for spring.

But even with all there was to do in the short daylight hours, Jack found time to think about Beth. Especially in the evenings before his tired body tumbled into bed.

One bitterly cold day, he realized that he hadn't thought about Cathy in many days. She couldn't come around much due to the weather. He was surprised he'd all but forgotten her, but that was fine with him. Besides, it was way too cold in one of the deserted barns to satisfy any itch he *might* have had for her.

Even though there were fewer chores, JT didn't let up about anything that didn't get done quick enough or to his satisfaction.

"Jack, did you check that fencing? And that hay baler needs looking at," he admonished.

"I'll *get* to it, JT." Jack gritted his teeth.

Or he'd bring up Beth.

"I was hoping for a Christmas engagement," JT badgered him one morning at breakfast.

When Jack didn't reply, JT suggested, "You could always get *her* pregnant. That'd be a way to get her to marry you."

Jack pushed his chair back from the table, thinking it was best to get after the chores instead of telling JT what he thought of that idea.

~~~~~~

Lucy, the mistress of fun, planned a trip to Chicago on President's Day in mid-February. We caught an early train, riding into the city with all the daily commuters. It might have been a school holiday, and banks were closed and no mail would be delivered, but offices were still open.

We visited the Art Institute first. Not Lucy's favorite, but certainly mine. We shopped at Field's, riding the escalator to each floor, gawking at all the displays. As a lark, we rode the express elevator to the top of the Prudential Building: Chicago's tallest building. Looking out, we could see Navy Pier sticking out into Lake Michigan, and in the other direction, overlooking the Loop, we noticed construction of a building that, based on the scaffolding, could easily eclipse this towering structure.

"Thanks, Lucy, for planning today and dragging me out," I told her on the train home.

"You got it bad, Liz," she teased. "I had to do something."

~~~~~~

February may have had fewer days than other months, but it sure took forever to turn into March. I was in a slump, which could only be remedied with a visit from Jack. However, during our phone calls, he didn't mention any plans to leave the ranch. I was upset with myself for getting so emotionally involved with this dark-haired, handsome, charming *stranger* and believing some kind of long-distance relationship could possibly work.

Lucy was making plans to visit Arizona over spring break and look for housing. What I needed to be doing was figuring out what I was going to do after graduation. In less than three months, I needed to have a plan. Stay here? Go back to the city to try and find some kind of job, some kind of work? Try and find a job here? Go on to graduate school here? Go to a different university for graduate work?

I hated to give up my dream of teaching. It was tempting to follow Lucy, but that was *her* plan, not mine. Going to grad school to pursue an advanced degree in Literature would be a waste of my time—and money, if I still couldn't find a job afterward.

Around and around my thoughts would spin without ever landing on one idea long enough for serious consideration.

Until I received two pieces of mail. One was a job offer at the local high school. Only temporary, teaching one semester this fall while the permanent teacher was out on maternity leave.

The other was an acceptance letter to the Graduate School in Arizona.

Grad school can wait. A teaching job! Maybe it could turn into something permanent.

I grabbed both envelopes and headed next door to share the news with Lucy.

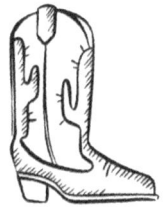

CHAPTER 9

Finally, the winter weather moderated in the Midwest, but probably not in Montana. The sun was out for longer moments each day and for more days in a row. The piles of snow were melting, and muddy ruts lined walkways where the snowplows had ripped into the grass. Boots were still necessary, but most days heavy winter coats could be traded for lighter-weight jackets. Students talked excitedly about travel plans to Florida or to a new destination called Cancun. Most midterm exams were taken and graded, and the long-anticipated spring break was just a week away.

Jack called to tell me he was coming for a visit. He could stay the entire week of break. Days, *and nights*, together. I was filled with anticipation.

~~~~~~

Jack's uncle picked him up from the airport this time as my last class on that Friday conflicted with his arrival time. When his uncle dropped him off at my apartment, I almost ran out to the curb to meet him. But, hearing my mother's voice yet again—"Elizabeth, don't be too eager. It's often said that men enjoy pursuing"—I waited until he knocked on the door.

After stepping inside, he crushed me to his frame and started kissing me passionately. Oh, those kisses. I had *almost* forgotten how overwhelming, how *overpowering* his kisses were. My legs turned to jelly and I staggered into him a bit. Jack took that as a definite green light and shrugged off his unbuttoned coat, one arm at a time, maintaining a firm embrace throughout.

"I've been waiting all day to do this," he said gruffly. "I want you, Beth." And with that, his hand moved down to cup my ass, pressing my lower body to his. I could feel his hardness through his jeans, and with one swift motion, he pinned me to the inside of the front door, nuzzling my neck with his furry face and groaning softly.

"Darlin', we sure have started something here." He broke off suddenly and gave me a gentle push toward the bedroom. Quickly he was next to me, stroking me, removing my blouse and jeans in one very experienced maneuver.

The sex was just like our earlier times, filled with passion and fireworks. And even though this first coupling quickly became "I was *ready* and he was *hard*" and lasted only a few fast strokes, it was intensely pleasurable.

Later, he retrieved his coat off the living room floor. In one of the deep pockets of what I called his *Marlboro Man* jacket—with the sheepskin collar and lining like the cowboy in the commercials—he pulled out a surprise present: a bottle of tequila and, amazingly, a couple of limes. Did he bring those all the way from Montana or stop on his way into town?

Combining shots and rock and roll, I didn't think our love-making could get *any* better. Jack's fingers and tongue would take me almost to the brink, and then he would ease me back down with playful kisses on my lips and breasts. When he finally entered me, the tequila had erased my remaining inhibitions; I wrapped my legs tightly around his lower backside and held on for an erotic ride. Hearts thumping, we quickly went flying together over the edge.

~~~~~~

Damn, the girl could fuck, Jack thought later. But it was *more* than that. He had awakened a passion in her, and not just from the tequila. She was so responsive to his kisses and fondling that when he finally couldn't wait to enter her, he found her wet and hot and tight. He had to control himself from going off like a teenage boy looking at naked women in *Playboy*. He had always enjoyed sex in college and since then, and before the holidays, he had especially had fun with Cathy. But with Beth, it was something *more*. And with a jolt, he realized he was *making love with* Beth instead of *putting his cock to* Cathy.

~~~~~~

For the next week, Jack and I saw each other as much as my studies would allow. I didn't have any classes to attend during the break, but there were still projects and papers to complete. There wasn't much I could do at this point to jeopardize my graduation, but I wasn't going to play *all* week and risk lowering my GPA in my very last semester.

I spent the mornings in the library, but Jack and I spent the afternoons walking around campus or going to the movies. His uncle was not out of town this time, so every *night* together was in my cramped apartment instead of the spacious old mansion.

~~~~~~

During one afternoon walk, we neared one of my favorite spots, the oldest building on campus. It was a four-story ornate limestone structure, complete with an arched entry, turrets, and gargoyles. The second level had dramatic floor-to-ceiling, stained-glass windows that overlooked a well-tended flower bed. Of course, this time of year, only the windows were impressive. Secreted to one side of the garden, under a sprawling flowering crab tree, there was a "lover's bench." As the legend goes, if you kiss your *true* love on this bench, you will soon marry and live happily ever after, just like in the fairy tales.

The spot was really quite pretty in *any* other season, but not the end of winter. Now, the tree's tangled branches were bare, and dead leaves poked out of the melting snow that covered the shady ground under the bench.

With his gloves, Jack brushed the frost and twigs off the bench and, looking at me expectantly, patted it with his hand. It was chilly and overcast, and I wasn't sure what he had in mind. But as he went down on one knee, he had a serious look on his face. Studying me with that intense stare I had grown to know, he started, "Darlin', I've thought about this since we parted in January. I've even prayed on it. And I want you for my wife. Will you marry me?"

Still on one knee, he pulled a small box from his deep coat pocket and, opening it, revealed the most beautiful, most unusual ring I'd ever seen. It was a delicate combination of gold filigree spun into a petal-like shape with a stunning blue stone anchored in the center. And just then, the sun filtered through the thin clouds and then through the bare branches and landed smack dab on that blue stone, illuminating it for a very long moment. In an electrifying instant, I saw that the stone's intense color was incredibly similar to Jack's dazzling blue eyes.

I looked at him with a mix of astonishment and apprehension.

"It was my grandma's ring, darlin', been in the family for

a long time, but I know she would be approving of this marriage. Please say yes."

I couldn't say this possibility had *never* crossed my mind, but I would always push those thoughts away. Moving to Montana was such a huge decision. It was so far away. I hardly knew the man. I'd only met Uncle Robert, not his father. I've never traveled out of my home state. I knew nothing about ranching, horses, or cows.

I was about to ask if I could think about it. And he might have read my thoughts, because when I looked at him, he once again used that penetrating stare to wear me down.

Here I was, about to cross that divide, with Jack on one knee, looking at me expectantly, hopefully. I remembered when I wanted to go out on New Year's Eve and all the times he would *tell* me he was driving my car. And how each time, he persuaded me to his will. I knew right then he would never take no for an answer.

Could I live with this strong-willed cowboy who would make all the decisions? I would be on a ranch, alone and knowing only him. The sex was incredible, but was that enough? Mom had cautioned me, more than once, that there was more to marriage than four feet in bed. Compromise. *Can I do that?*

To be honest, I had fallen in love with this handsome Montana man. I believed that he would be not only my lover and my partner, but also my protector and my champion.

"Yes, I *will* marry you, Jack." And with those few words, my boring, simple life was changed forever.

He pulled off my mitten and slipped the ring on my finger. Should I have been surprised that it fit perfectly? In one motion, he rose, scooped me off the bench, and crushed me to him in those powerful, strong arms.

"Darlin', you've made me one happy man. Now let's get out of this cold and somewhere warm where I'll make you one happy woman." His eyes had a wicked gleam, but then he winked, and I couldn't help but laugh.

~~~~~~

Over and over again, I made Jack describe Montana in general, and the ranch in particular, in great detail. Most times he'd say, "Well, darlin', it's big. And open. And you can see just about forever. The mountains are way off in the distance. And then there's that big sky. And the air smells so fresh. And you can see a billion stars at night. Oh, I know you'll love it there. It's the prettiest place on Earth."

But once, he told me, "Beth, I won't lie to you. Sometimes the huge empty plains and prairies can be the loneliest spot you'd ever care to be. And when the wind just howls and the snow blows so fierce, you think winter will never end." As he told me that, there was sadness in his eyes that I'd never noticed before.

I guess I thought we would marry in Montana, but Jack insisted we get married here—and soon; right after graduation. When I questioned him on this, he said, "Well, darlin', it's like this. I want us *married* when I bring you back home. I'm afraid if we wait until you're in Montana, you might change your mind. Besides, there are too many good-looking, young-stud ranch hands about the place and I'm afraid you'll take one look at them and then plumb forget about me," he added with a wink.

"But what about your father? I haven't met him, and he hasn't met me. Wouldn't he want us to get married in Montana?"

"Darlin', a trip here would just be too difficult to him." I started to ask why but then he added, "He's getting up in years, and we've found it best if only one of us is away from the ranch at the same time. Dad trusts my judgment *on this*. And my uncle has talked to him. *He's* met you. Besides, I've told JT *all* about you. You are *all* I talk about, day in and day out, back at the ranch."

"Good grief, I hope you haven't told them *everything* about me?" I blushed.

"Well, I did leave out that you especially like it when I tickle your inner thighs with my beard, and then there was that thing you did to me the other day in the shower, but other than that…"

I aimed a punch at his upper arm, but he turned slightly into my movement and I ended up in those vise-like arms.

"Don't worry, darlin'. Everything will be fine. My dad will love you just as much as I do."

And he proceeded to remind me just how much he loved me.

~~~~~~

When Jack told Beth that he talked about her "all the time" back at the ranch, that wasn't the truth. He justified lying to her because he didn't want her to change her mind about marrying him or delay the wedding with a long engagement. For some reason, even with that ring on her finger, he believed he had to keep up the charm.

~~~~~~

In a saner moment that week, I had a full-fledged panic attack about getting married in two months. What in the world had I agreed to? *I've never been to Montana. I haven't ridden a horse since I was a kid at summer camp. I've never seen a ranch.* And although Jack made Montana sound like the most beautiful place in the world, he did say it was empty plains and lonely prairies. *What about the Windy City and all the museums and art galleries I would visit every chance I got? And were there other women on the ranch?*

Would I be surrounded by big burly men who worked the ranch? What had I done?

Jack wanted our wedding on the day after graduation. But as persuasive as Jack could be, I held firm for the weekend after commencement. He reluctantly gave in, with the compromise that we'd head for Montana the Monday afterward and *honeymoon* on the road.

"Very romantic," I told him sarcastically.

He had pulled me to him and roughly kissed me, plundering my mouth with his tongue and erasing all my thoughts. I let him take me, consume me, and when I was fully under his spell, I had no choice but to agree.

~~~~~~

The next day was Sunday, and Jack was going back to Montana. His uncle had invited us both to his house for Saturday dinner. It was a quiet dinner, just the three of us, and at first, I was terribly shy. As Jack was spending all his nights with me, his uncle had to know we were sleeping together. I was nervous and embarrassed until I realized he wasn't judging me for my indiscretions with Jack. Between the wine and his uncle asking about my classes and our wedding plans, I soon relaxed.

"Dr. Juddson," I started.

"Beth, please call me Robert, or Uncle Robert, if you'd like."

"Uncle Robert," I started again. "Why didn't you stay in Montana? On the ranch?"

There was a long pause, and I blushed, thinking I'd asked too personal of a question. I looked to Jack, who was studying his uncle.

"Beth, I left the farm and enlisted to fight in the Korean War, as maybe Jack has told you. So it was like the song, 'How ya gonna keep 'em home, after they've seen the lights of Paree,'" he misquoted. "When I got back, I still wanted to travel. See a few more places on this earth, before we blew it up in the next war. I would never have that freedom on the ranch. Ranching is hard, full-time work, as Jack will attest. It's not for everyone," Robert finished.

Was he trying to talk me out of moving to Montana? No freedom to travel?

I looked at Jack, and he just winked.

Before Jack and I left to go back to my apartment, Uncle Robert asked, "Beth, would you like to ride along to the airport tomorrow?"

"Yes," I answered enthusiastically. *A few more hours with Jack*, I thought. But, remembering my manners, I quickly added, "Thank you for inviting me."

His uncle appeared to be honestly happy for Jack, and it was then that I knew he approved of me.

~~~~~

Our lovemaking that night was tender and sweet and long and slow. It was like we were trying to imprint the memory of our pleasuring so we could recall it when needed to help get through the next six weeks without each other.

I didn't care if Jack's uncle could see the passion in our goodbyes at the gate. Jack held me until the last possible minute before boarding. I tried not to cry as we left the terminal and headed to the car. After some attempts at small talk on the way back, his uncle left me to my own jumbled thoughts and bruised emotions as he pretended to concentrate on the traffic and driving.

CHAPTER 10

On the flight home, Jack's thoughts lingered on his feelings for Beth. He reminded himself *again* how lucky he was and how differently a pursuit such as this could have gone. And then he would dwell on the difficult but necessary conversation he needed to have with Cathy. He imagined all of her various reactions: hurt, anger, denial. There would be tears *and* cursing. He dreaded the confrontation and kept putting it off. But he had to face her soon.

Not one to put off unpleasant tasks, Jack always thought that just made the task harder. Best to get it out of the way. But he *had* been dragging his boots on this one. So the very next time Cathy came sashaying to the ranch, he told her they needed to talk. He thought it best to have this difficult conversation away from the ranch, and ranch *hands*, so he saddled up his horse and they rode off toward the privacy of the hills.

It was a sunny day, but the ground was still muddy and there were patches of snow here and there. They rode in silence for a while, just enjoying the early spring day. He was sure that Cathy figured he was taking her to one of the hay-storage outbuildings for some one-on-one. It *had* been a while since their last time. But that was the *last* thing on his mind, *and* his dick.

He was headed for a small rock cropping in the distance. One of the smaller rocks was quite smooth and you could comfortably sit on it. They loosely tethered the horses and, after checking for rattlesnakes, perched up on the rock.

"Okay, cowboy, don't expect me to be on the bottom. I'm not getting my butt pumiced on this rock," Cathy told him before Jack could start his not-so-rehearsed speech.

He planned to break it to her gently. He didn't intend to just blurt it out. He wanted to soften it...but how? By telling her they could continue as before? He knew her morals were loose enough to say *yes* to that arrangement. But he didn't really want to continue fucking Cathy while making love to Beth. But even as he told himself that, he wasn't sure he entirely believed it.

He'd been fucking Cathy for so long; it was almost like they *were* married. But they both knew that his old man, the great JT Juddson, would never allow a marriage between a girl like Cathy and his son. Just another reason Jack and his father would never see eye to eye—on anything, it seemed.

Cathy was a crazy, wild woman. She did outrageous things. Stunts. Many of a sexual nature. Like the time he came home from college in Bozeman for the weekend and a bunch of them went to the bar in town. Cathy was drinking heavily and while gyrating around on the dance floor decided to take her top off. Thankfully she had a very pretty bra on underneath, but still...

Another time, when leaving the bar, there was a local cop car parked on the curb outside. Cathy took one giant step up onto the trunk of the car then another giant step onto the roof. The third big step was a hop over the light bar and onto the hood and the fourth was a perfect dismount back to the sidewalk. If she knew that Bud was sitting in the car the whole time, she didn't care. Bud jumped out, saw who it was, checked the car for damage, and, seeing none, just told Jack to take her home. Jack hated to admit it, but some of those stunts were an incredible turn-on for him.

Without any introduction or explanation, he simply said, "I'm getting married in May."

He thought she would be surprised and maybe momentarily speechless. He thought she might shout and swear. But he never thought she would *laugh*.

"You're a little early for April Fool's, JJ." She burst out laughing. "But that sure is a good one."

"No, it's not a joke, Cathy. I met her last fall, and we were recently engaged and the wedding is set for early May."

"Well, that was pretty damn fast. Who the hell is she?"

"You don't know her. She's from back east. I met her when I was helping my uncle with his house," he lied. Well, *parts* of that were true.

She was quiet for a brief moment then the storm started. "So wait, you shit, you've been fucking us both?" she screamed at Jack. She was about to launch herself at him, but Jack jumped down from the rock. A second later, Cathy followed. "So, were you?"

Jack did not want to share one single intimate detail of Beth with Cathy. So, he just said, "No."

"No what? No, you haven't fucked her yet, or no, not both of us?" Then she was quiet, and he could see her thought process working in her eyes and on her face. "I see," was all she said. Then, just as quickly, she said, "Well, you could... I mean, we could...things don't have to change..."

He again said, "No."

He saw the hurt and then the anger when she yelled, "All those times together and, stupid me, I thought you'd eventually have the balls to stand up to your father. Fuck. I shoulda gotten knocked up, then you woulda hadta marry me."

And with that, she untangled the reins of her sorrel, threw her foot in the stirrup and her other leg over the saddle, and spurred the poor horse into a gallop away from Jack.

Jack had *never* really wanted to marry Cathy, and even if he did, did she really think his dad would allow it?

~~~~~~

Lucy was visibly shocked and uncharacteristically quiet when I told her my news and showed her the ring and asked if she would be my maid of honor.

"Liz, you hardly know the man!" she finally exclaimed. "Besides being a stud in the bedroom, what else do you know about him? It's been, what? Seven months? And long-distantly at that. At least delay the wedding for a while. Visit Montana and the ranch."

"I suggested that. He wants to marry as soon as possible. Right after graduation."

"But Liz, you're not even sure about how you met Jack. Remember the photo? And what about the class schedule you found in his dresser?"

"Lucy, we explained all of that. The picture was in the yearbook. And after we met, his uncle probably printed my schedule for Jack. That all made sense, remember?"

"What about the job offer to teach? Your dream."

"I'll get a job in Montana. I'm sure there are schools out there too," I added sarcastically.

"At least live with him in Montana before you commit to marriage."

"I don't think that would go over with his father, Lucy. They all live together on the ranch."

"Just postpone the wedding. Take the teaching job for the fall."

All good advice. All things I had considered and then discarded. I *loved* Jack. So why wait? Jack was smart and funny. He believed in God and was a hard worker. He would take care of me. And I knew he would never hit me or treat me poorly. One time on the phone, he told me that he had just fired one of the ranch hands. He said he didn't particularly care for that part of the job, but they just wouldn't tolerate certain behavior on the ranch. When I questioned him about *what* kind of behavior, he said "disrespecting women." I asked what the ranch hand had done. Jack told me, "He'd gotten liquored up and slapped his girlfriend around. Gave her a black eye."

~~~~~~

The next few weeks raced by. I swam as often as I could in between classes and end-of-semester projects, making it all work in my mind as my body plowed the water. But I still alternated between Lucy's questions and my own: What was I doing?

Is Lucy right? Should I wait? If I give up this teaching job, will there be another in Montana? Will I be able to use my degree or were the last four years a waste of hard work and money? Is there really no freedom on the ranch? Why is Jack in such a hurry to marry me?

And then Jack would call and tell me how much he missed me and how he couldn't wait until we were married, and once again I'd convince myself this *was* the right decision. Montana wasn't *that* far away, right? At times I could *almost* get excited about living on a ranch. Jack's vivid descriptions made that part of the country sound breathtaking. My boring life wouldn't be boring anymore. And now I had a plan for after graduation.

Jack called a couple of times a week and then every day the week before he returned.

One time, I told him I was worried about his long-distance

bill and suggested that it was only fair that occasionally I should call *him*.

But he laughed and said, "Now, darlin', don't *you* be worrying about the telephone bills."

And before I could argue any further, just like always, he changed the subject by asking me if I was behaving myself.

"Yes, of course," I told him and then volleyed back, "And what about you?"

He laughed again and told me he was saving himself for marriage.

CHAPTER 11

Jack came out three weeks before the wedding. When he stepped inside my apartment, I pulled his head down and kissed him as passionately as I had at the airport.

"Oh, I missed you," we both said at the same time when we came up for air. And then we both laughed.

There was so much to do before graduation. I had one more project to finish, which meant more hours in the library. And I needed to study for final exams. I would have trouble doing that with Jack underfoot. Or on top of me.

"Are you staying with your uncle?" I shyly asked.

"Yes, darlin'. I know you have that last push for the end of the semester. Believe it or not, I do remember."

Something else I had to do, but had been putting off, was write a letter to the local school district to turn down the temporary teaching job. When I suggested to Jack that we postpone the wedding by a few months so I could take the job, he was uncompromising on the date.

"But Jack, having some—even a little—teaching experience will help me find another teaching job in Montana."

He said nothing to that. Instead, he told me, "We need to

be in Montana before it snows."

"Maybe we could be apart for a month so I could finish out the semester."

"Absolutely not!" he retorted with a tone that indicated the subject was closed.

~~~~~~

There was a long list of things we needed for the wedding. We had to go over to the next town, where the County Courthouse was, to apply for a marriage license. Blood tests had to be scheduled and taken. And we needed to buy wedding bands.

"Beth, will you be happy with simple gold bands?" Jack asked me as he pulled a small box from his pocket. "You have the blue ring for sparkle," he added.

Surprised that he'd already bought them, having always imagined a diamond wedding ring, I wondered if it really mattered.

The small box held both rings: one large and the other much smaller. An intricate scrollwork patterned each thick gold band, making them anything but plain or simple.

"They're stunning, Jack," I told him honestly.

Lucy helped me find a dress. For several Saturdays, we rummaged through every resale shop in the small downtown area.

"Liz, this is it!" Lucy shouted excitedly. She held up a beautiful vintage dress. It was long and ivory-colored. It had lace on the bodice and skirting.

"Oh, that's beautiful. How much is it?" I asked.

She read the tag. "Only thirty dollars. Try it on," she suggested.

There were a half-dozen fabric-covered buttons that fastened the dress in the back, but I could only reach the top three. Lucy would have to button the others as I fantasized about Jack unbuttoning them. I might have worried about his thick fingers if he hadn't successfully opened the clasp on my horseshoe necklace.

The dress had a high neckline. Pushing my hair into a messy updo, I could imagine how that would emphasize my height even more. The bodice tapered to a fitted waistline, which hugged me perfectly, while the lace skirting, with its uniquely scalloped edging, fell to the middle of my calf.

"Oh, Liz," Lucy exclaimed as I stepped out of the dressing room. "It's perfect. And it definitely qualifies as your 'something old,'" she reminded me, giggling.

~~~~~~

Jack's uncle knew a non-denominational minister who would marry us in the tiny chapel of the Congregational Church. It would be a very small gathering with a private ceremony. Lucy and his uncle would be our witnesses, and the four of us would have dinner afterward at the fanciest restaurant in this little college town. Jack promised that we would host a big reception party after I got settled in Montana. Lucy would be invited to fly up and stay a few days.

Once all the wedding plans were taken care of, I buckled down to finish my last project for school and study for exams. With all the late nights at the library, I didn't see much of Jack the week before graduation.

On Friday night, Lucy and I paraded around my apartment, showing off our "academic regalia" to Jack. It almost didn't seem real to me. Mom's dream for me actually coming true.

~~~~~~

Lucy's huge family was coming for graduation. Other than Jack, there would be no one else in the audience for me, but

I decided to walk anyway, and Lucy, being Lucy, insisted on a BIG party after the ceremony. We had planned the menu, pooled our resources, and were totally prepared for the Big Day. The weather cooperated. It was warm, but not too hot. And not a drop of rain in the forecast.

Saturday morning was a blur. What with Lucy's family arriving in shifts and last-minute preparations for the party, the time to leave for our ceremony in the University Center was finally here. Jack and I squeezed into one of the several carloads of Lucy's family.

Having different majors, Lucy and I couldn't sit together for the ceremony. The proceedings dragged on. The speeches were long. Each college dean said a few words. Then the university president said some longer words. Lastly, the campus minister led a prayer and blessed us all.

It was finally time to walk and get the coveted sheepskin, which in reality was an empty diploma cover. The dean of each college read their students' names. Each graduate walked across the stage to an isolated round of applause, shouts, and whistles from their family.

As I walked across the stage, I knew that Lucy's family would make some noise, but above all that was a loud, piercing wolf whistle followed by chuckles from the rest of the audience.

Amazingly, I didn't stumble, but I did blush. As the dean shook my hand and handed me the "diploma," he winked and whispered, "Someone out there appreciates you, Elizabeth."

Smiling to myself as I left the stage, I thought, *Yes. Yes, he does!*

After everyone had walked and caps were flung toward the ceiling, it took a while for the auditorium to empty. I tried to find Lucy and her family in the congested lobby. Someone jostled me and then grabbed my arm. I turned to see and there was Jack, pulling me into those familiar arms and crushing me to his hard body.

"Congratulations, Beth. One ceremony down. One to go." And then those arresting blue eyes gave me that knowing wink.

~~~~~~

Jack had agreed to help out at the party, mainly with some of the bartending tasks—keeping ice in the big tub of beer, changing out the empty keg for a new one. But all the time, he was close to me—either literally, with his arm possessively around me, or figuratively, with his piercing stares.

Finally, after a couple of hours, the party wound down, and we decided it was safe to sneak next door. The door had hardly closed behind us before we set upon each other, unbuttoning and unzipping, leaving a pile of clothes just inside the door. Jack kissed my mouth, then my neck, while his hands roamed freely over my body, pausing to stroke his thumbs over my nipples, causing a flutter lower down. Boldly, my hand snaked down to feel his manhood, hard as steel and hot as sin. His shaft jerked slightly as my fingers tried to encircle its girth. He made a guttural, unintelligible sound as he maneuvered me against the wall. With our fingers interlaced, I could only squirm with pleasure as he pinned my arms and proceeded to suckle to hardness one nipple and then the other. His tongue flicked and swirled before he very gently nibbled the rigid tip.

With his beard brushing my breasts, I melted from the sensations. My knees were weak and I feared I would slide down the wall to the floor, reduced to a puddle at his feet. But he was well aware of the effects of his ministrations and pulled back, moving up to nuzzle my neck, kissing my earlobe, then finally taking my mouth, plunging his tongue to its depth while pressing the length of him against me. My recovery was short-lived because soon he was pressing his hand to my mound, fingers parting my folds, searching for my center. His fingers slipped inside, finding the slickness that told him I was ready. Seizing the moment, he guided me to the floor and, stretching out above me, slid the entire length of him into me with one fluid motion. My legs wrapped around his, and we were once again lost in the pleasure of each other's body.

When he thought I could walk again, he helped me off the floor and steered me toward the bedroom and the comfort of the bed. The next time was slower, sweeter, but just as passionate. He teased me until I thought I would have to beg him to mount me. My orgasm was only a precursor to his.

Lying in his arms afterward, I thought, *He sure knows exactly what to do and exactly where to touch me.* Did I want to know about his past? How he had learned to please a woman so well? I wasn't a virgin the first time we slept together, and he knew that. Perhaps, I thought, it was best to not explore ancient history.

He wasn't sleeping, but he had a drowsy, sexy look about him. We snuggled together naked, touching each other, not so much to arouse but to continue the closeness that only intimacy can bring.

"I'm hungry," Jack announced. "And a beer would be nice," he added.

We retrieved our scattered clothing and went back next door to Lucy's for leftovers. Luckily, her parents and older relatives had gone back to their hotels, and the friends remaining were pretty well hammered and didn't notice our glow.

The weekend passed way too fast. The next day, Lucy's folks and her brother packed all the cars and headed home. Lucy would follow after the wedding. Jack and I walked around campus in the afternoon and had dinner with his uncle that evening.

~~~~~~

The week after graduation and before the wedding, we still had to figure out what to do with all my stuff. Most of my furniture was early college crap. Putting it out on the curb for the next owner was the best option. I had sorted and packed most of my clothes. Many boxes of books were taped and labeled. The dishes and kitchen things were another dilemma.

"Beth, if you have anything of your mother's that has a sentimental value, let's pack it up. Everything else, donate it."

"There are a few pieces," I told him. I planned to cook for Jack using her casserole dish, her angel food cake pan, and, of course, her recipes.

The big strike issue was my car. Jack wanted me to sell it.

"But I don't *want* to sell my car," I argued. It wasn't new, but it was my last vestige of independence. And my freedom. Without a car, I couldn't run into town. Did "town" in Montana even have a library?

"It not a practical vehicle for the rough ranch roads, darlin'." I started to protest, but seeing that thought on my face, he quickly added, "Beth, you'll bust the oil pan for sure and possibly even break the axle hitting a rut. You'll have to learn how to drive one of the pickup trucks."

It was settled in his mind, but not mine. We finally compromised by leaving my car in his uncle's garage for the time being.

"Maybe my uncle could drive it out later in the summer. Or maybe we could come back for it in the fall," he suggested.

"Maybe homecoming weekend?" I asked.

"Uhmm, we'll see, Beth."

~~~~~~

Our wedding day started off rainy, but by midday the sun was shining and it was as near-perfect a spring day as you can get at this time of year in this part of the Midwest. Jack had insisted on staying at his uncle's the last several nights. We had been "celibate" for that entire time. It wasn't that we hadn't gone longer without having each other; it just had never happened when we'd been in the same state.

Lucy lent me a lacy handkerchief to carry as my "borrowed" item and Jack presented me with a beautiful turquoise bracelet the day before our wedding, so I counted that as both the "something new" and the "something blue." My heart was sad that my mother was not here to see this day. First my college graduation and now my wedding. *Oh, Mom, I miss you.*

Jack wore a rented tux and looked so very handsome. My heart fluttered as I walked toward him from the back of the chapel. For sure, I was a lucky woman. Those blue eyes locked onto mine and, like a magnet, tugged me down the aisle. When he wasn't undressing me with his penetrating stare, I believed he could see all the way into my soul.

"Jackson Lawrence Juddson, do you take this woman, Elizabeth Sarah Mitchell, to be your lawfully wedded wife, to honor and to hold, to love and to cherish, in sickness and in health, from this day forward until death do you part?"

"I do," he firmly stated.

"And Elizabeth Sarah Mitchell, do you take this man, Jackson Lawrence Juddson, to be your lawfully wedded husband, to honor and *obey*, to love and cherish, in sickness and in health, from this day forward until death do you part?"

"I do," I softly replied.

"With the power vested in me, and before God and these witnesses, I pronounce you man and wife. Jackson, you may kiss your bride."

And with that, Jack bent his head and kissed me ever so gently. Brushing his cheek against mine, he whispered in my ear, "I love you, Beth, but if I kiss you any longer or harder, I'll have to *have* you right here, on the floor, 'before God and all these witnesses.'"

Oh, that man could make me blush.

After the legal paperwork was signed and an offering was surrendered to the minister, the four of us piled into Lucy's car and headed to Ricardo's Ranch on the eastern edge of town. The oldest and fanciest restaurant in the area, Ricardo's had been around for decades. The original Ricardo migrated out from Chicago, but the rumors around him remained: that he was "connected" to the Chicago mob, that Al Capone had dined there several times, and that even Richard J. Daley had enjoyed Ricardo's famous prime rib.

Paneled in a rich, dark mahogany, you walked on thick, plush carpets when escorted to your table in one of the many intimate dining rooms that made up the sprawling restaurant. Not only did they bring you a bread basket, but also a relish tray. All dinners were four-course meals: starting with tomato juice or soup, then a salad or cottage cheese, followed by your entrée with a choice of five different types of potatoes, and, at the end, one of their fabulous homemade desserts.

College students couldn't afford to eat at Ricardo's, but if one was lucky enough to have parents or relatives treat them, they had leftovers for several meals.

Jack's uncle ordered a bottle of champagne, and toasts were made by both his uncle and Lucy. Despite our small group, but perhaps due to our wedding attire, the host and the waiter made a fuss over us. We were even treated to a second bottle of bubbly. Jack's uncle had arranged for a small wedding cake. Between the food and the company, I was quite content. Alternating between happy and excited, I was confident in my love for Jack and blessed with Lucy's dear friendship. I was eager to see the sights on our road trip to Montana and looking forward to sharing a life with Jack. But try as I might, I could not ignore the twinge of sadness that my mom had missed this special day and would never get to meet Jack.

Lucy dropped Jack's uncle off at the church where he'd left

his car, and then the three of us went back to the apartment building. Lucy begged off to finish packing, but I saw the wink she gave Jack.

Taking care with Jack's rented tux and the fabric-covered buttons on my vintage dress, our lovemaking was slow and tender. It might have lacked the fireworks of previous times, but it was very satisfying. And there were repeat performances throughout the night.

CHAPTER 12

We left early in the morning that following Monday for the drive to Montana. Jack had packed the truck the day before while I helped Lucy pack her car. Lucy and I hugged each other and she said to me, "Liz, I hope you'll be happy on that ranch. And if that cowboy steps out of line, you just let me know."

"Oh, Lucy, he won't. He loves me. Now remember, you promised you'd come to Montana for the reception later this summer."

"And I will. Just let me know when. Girl, you know I *never* turn down a party invitation. Even if have to cross the country to get there."

~~~~~~

Jack said it would take us several days, maybe a week, to get to the ranch. There were some places he wanted to show me along the way, he said.

"Like what?" I asked.

"Oh, every motel room between here and there." He grinned wickedly.

I was just happy to be with him. Full-time. Every day. And *every* night. No more being apart. And no more long-distance telephone conversations. I rode, sitting in the middle of the truck's bench seat, pressed up against Jack. Often, he drove one-handed with his arm around me. Other times, I would have my hand on his neck, playing with his hair, with his hand tucked between my thighs. When the sun would glint off my new gold wedding band, I would smile. One time, I even giggled out loud.

"Ticklish?" he asked, his hand tightening on my leg, threatening to move farther up my thigh.

"No—well, yes, but I was remembering what…er, we did at the motel last night."

I still was way too shy to *talk* about sex, but I was getting bolder about *doing* things during our lovemaking. Just last night, I had brazenly gripped his naked erection and then tentatively explored the fascinating ridges and veins with my fingertips. His penis twitched and jumped in my hand. It was so much fun to discover its secrets. And it was mine, to play with. Thinking about it made me blush, but it also made me giggle. Did every bride feel this way?

But, of course, I didn't tell Jack *any* of that. I just mumbled how happy I was and that brought a smile to *his* face.

~~~~~~

Jack was determined to get through Iowa that first day. No offense, Iowa, but it didn't look a great deal different than Illinois. Mile after mile of corn fields, only broken up by a soybean or wheat field here and there. We took the interstate where we could, but Jack preferred the more rural routes. We would catch FM radio stations when we were near cities of any size. Then we would sing along to Bobby McGee, Maggie May, and American Pie. We stopped for lunch at a diner in one of those small farm towns somewhere in the middle of the state. Everyone turned to look at us when we walked through the door. But with Jack's cowboy hat and boots, I guessed folks figured he was okay. No one ever hassled us.

The first night, we stopped south of Sioux City and stayed at a roadside place called the Cedar Tree Motel. I told Jack that it reminded me of the Bates Motel in *Psycho*. He told me that the only *stabbing* that would take place would be with a certain member of his anatomy to a certain part of mine. But he insisted that we shower together. Just in case.

The second day was more fun as, by midmorning, we were making the first stop at one of the places Jack wanted to show me. We stopped in Mitchell, South Dakota, to see the famous Corn Palace. Looking like something from Zanzibar with its minarets and onion domes, the building was entirely decorated in corn.

"This really belongs in Iowa," I exclaimed.

"Well, darlin', there's an argument that the *first* corn palace *was* in Iowa. But this is the only one now."

We stayed there for a while and learned that there were at least twelve different shades of corn and over two hundred thousand ears of corn used to create the murals on the outside of the building. The murals changed every year because "Actually, darlin', it's one big bird feeder," Jack informed me.

We pushed on to the next surprise destination, but I guessed it long before we got there. Of course, all the signs advertising it for miles sure helped: Wall Drug Store. More than just a drugstore, it was a shopper's dream. Jack stayed right next to me so he could pull me out of there before I went crazy. The truck was pretty much crammed full of my stuff, so we didn't have a lot of room for souvenirs, but he did let me buy a T-shirt, two mugs, and a magnet.

"Jack, besides the great sex, I needed a few *things* to commemorate my honeymoon," I reasoned with him.

We weren't too far from the last place he wanted to share with me—Mount Rushmore. He thought it best to find a motel and then tackle the famous landmark the next day. After my comments about the Cedar Tree Motel, he found a Holiday Inn where we would spend the next two nights.

~~~~~~

Mother Nature smiled upon us and gave us a beautiful spring day to spend in the park. Of course, I'd seen pictures of the massive carvings. Wall Drug Store had postcards showing every possible view: up close, far away, sunny blue skies, storm clouds hovering, and even some with snow. And who could forget the climactic ending of Hitchcock's *North by Northwest* where Cary Grant hauled Eva Marie Saint from the precipice?

However, seeing the enormous faces of these early leaders of our great country...well, it just gave me goosebumps.

After viewing the giant faces from every angle we could, we hiked along the trails, enjoying the spring day and stretching our legs after two days in the truck. Jack carried a cooler and I carried a sleeping bag. Since it was early in the season and during the week, we were nearly the only hikers in the park. We found a secluded but sunny glade where we could have our picnic lunch. After sandwiches and cold beers that he smuggled in, we stretched out on top of the unzipped sleeping bag and enjoyed the sun.

It was very dangerous for the two of us to be alone on a blanket in reclining positions. I don't remember who started kissing who, but soon Jack was tugging on my T-shirt and pushing his hand up inside it. His hands were cool and the chill of his fingers instantly aroused my nipples. *That* response encouraged him to expose my entire breast to his mouth for a proper suckling. Even as our desire increased, I could not fully relax, and when he tried to unbutton my jeans, I held him back.

"What? Married three days and had enough of me already?" He smirked.

"Of course not! But I've never done *it* outside. Can't we go back to the motel?"

He just smiled and continued to tease me. Kissing me to stem any further verbal protests, he managed to get my jeans unbuttoned and his hand down my pants. His hand was between my jeans and my panties, but I knew in just a matter of time he would be touching bare skin.

He must have sensed my continued reluctance or maybe he heard something; I didn't know for sure. But he *didn't* go inside my panties and, although he continued to kiss me, he zipped up my jeans and pulled my T-shirt down. His kisses were still tender, but not urgent, and he rolled on his side, bringing me with him, holding me pressed to the length of his body.

"My little city girl," he teased.

~~~~~~

Within two hours of starting out the next morning and after cutting through the corner of Wyoming, we were finally in Montana! In contrast to the flat landscape of Illinois and Iowa, this terrain got lumpier the farther west we traveled. Round, undulating mounds covered the earth like giant, grass-covered ant hills. In the valleys of the mounds, you couldn't see around or over the next one. I had never seen rounded hills like these before, and *so many*, just mile after mile of them. Buttes and bluffs were visible in the distance. Rock outcroppings were scattered here and there among those rolling hills, like a giant had haphazardly dropped stones on his travels.

And always, those mountains teased me on the horizon.

I could now understand the "Big Sky" moniker. The sky *did* seem bigger. Was it because of the acres and acres of open, undeveloped land? But it was also so empty and desolate. Of course, I didn't say *any* of this to Jack. We would drive for miles without seeing any kind of building or structure. And not many trees. But there *were* hundreds of bales of hay. As we kept driving, I wondered to myself what the ranch would be like. And I hated to even *think* it, but I wondered if I'd made a mistake. My first impression of Montana was that it was lonely. Big sky and wide-open spaces, but no buildings, trees, or people. And how could you possibly drive a truck around all those dips and rises?

A little after midday, we were nearing Billings, and Jack asked me if I wanted to stop for lunch or press on to Bozeman, where we were going to stay for several days. Maybe a week, he said.

"A week!" I cried. "Are you postponing introducing me to your father?"

I think he thought I was serious because he suddenly jerked the truck over to the side of the road, slammed on the brakes, and turned off the ignition. Turning to me, he said, "Beth, I love you, darlin'. We just need to spend a few days in Bozeman to do some shopping. And besides, this is *our* honeymoon and I'd sure like it to last as long as possible," he added with that lascivious look of his. "Once we get back to the ranch...well, I'll be busy. Spring is one of the busiest times with calving and getting the hay planted and checking fences..."

Before he could continue rattling off all the ranch chores, I put my arms around him and kissed him. I loved him *so* much right then. All my negative thoughts about Montana evaporated.

~~~~~~

We stayed at the Cattleman's Inn in Bozeman. The "Inn," as Jack called it, was one of the oldest hotels in town, but it had been totally renovated, so it was also the nicest. Upon checking in, the desk clerk said, "Welcome back, Mr. Juddson."

I wanted to question Jack about the clerk knowing him so well, but once we got to the room, the bed was too inviting for us. *Afterward*, we took a shower and got dressed for dinner. I finally remembered to ask him when we were downstairs in the restaurant, ordering cold beer and steaks.

"Well, darlin', we make it down to Bozeman every month, month and a half, and we always stay here."

"Who's *we*?" I asked innocently.

He seemed puzzled at first by my question. He said, "Anyone who comes down from the ranch. Dad or Glenn. Usually a ranch hand or two." Then he understood the point of my question and grinned. He took my hand and said, "Beth, have I told you today that I love you, darlin'?" He brought my hand to his lips, turned it palm-up, and kissed the center of my hand.

I got a tingle all the way to my...well, eventually, my toes. That man had a way about him. He knew *exactly* what to say and do, and *exactly* at the right moment.

~~~~~~

We spent the next two days sightseeing around Bozeman. He took me to Pompey's Pillar, a huge sandstone rock formation, where Clark, of the famous *Lewis and Clark*, had inscribed his name. Jack also took me to the Little Bighorn Battlefield National Monument, which of course commemorated the famous Indian battle with Custer. Having gone to college in Bozeman, Jack had seen both of those famous sites, probably many times and probably with different co-eds. But I pushed aside my jealousy and tried to be impressed with the historical significance of both places.

The next morning, he took me shopping at Donnoly's, famous for its Western wear and tack. Jack tried to explain that "tack" referred in general to all of the numerous bridles, bits, reins, and saddles one needed to ride a horse. According to Jack, Donnoly's would have every Western piece of clothing I would need. Looking around the impressive store, it sure looked like they did. I didn't think I needed much, maybe some boots. But Jack said, "Oh no, you need much more than that." I was bewildered and not sure how to approach this shopping expedition. With Jack's uncanny ability to read my mind, he said with that charming grin, "Think of it as your trousseau, darlin'."

"Oh Jack, how...old-fashioned," I blurted out, laughing. It was the first thing that popped into my head.

Once again, he was greeted by name, this time by one of the owners. In no time, I was trying on jeans and boots, jackets and hats. I even got gloves and bandanas. By the time we left, they all had done their best to make a cowgirl out of me. Well, at least I could *dress* like one now.

We spent another day just goofing around, mainly in the hotel. *Specifically* in our room. Our lovemaking rivaled that of earlier times and I was always amazed by not only his stamina but also by his insatiable desire. And his ability to transport me to that state of intense, unbelievable pleasure time after time. I had never been so happy and so in love.

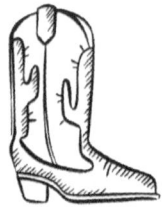

CHAPTER 13

Finally, it was time to take me to the ranch. We headed north and east of Bozeman and drove through towns with descriptive names like Spring Rock and Willow Mound. Road signs pointed to other towns such as Bark Creek and Forest Grove. We crossed North Fork Creek, Ferry Creek, and Fox Creek. At Bear Canyon Road, we left the striped county highway and took a barely paved township road that eventually turned into a gravel road called Big Elm Tree Road. I briefly wondered where the large elm tree was since there wasn't a tree in sight. Several miles after that, the gravel road became two rutted grooves through the prairie grass. Every so often, Jack would have to stop the truck and get out to open a gate.

After the third time, I asked him, "Why are there so many closed gates out in the middle of nowhere?"

"Darlin', it's because of the cattle."

"Jack, what cattle? There's not a cow in sight," I said, straining to look as far as my eyes could see.

"Well, not right now, but later in the summer there will be cattle. It's just a way of life out here, Beth," he offered as an explanation. "You'll get used to it."

At the very next gate, I got out of the truck and asked him to show me how to open and close it.

"I'd like to help," I told him when he raised an eyebrow.

After going through several more gates, I asked him, "Where are we? Whose land *is* this?"

"Well, darlin', this is Juddson land," he proudly declared.

"This is your ranch?" I exclaimed. I had *never* imagined it was this huge. I thought it was like the size of a large farm back home. "How *big* is it?"

"I don't suppose the actual numbers of acres would mean much to you, Beth," he teased, "so I'll just tell you that if you look about ten miles in any direction, you're on the ranch."

I was a city girl, but nothing had prepared me for this experience. I could hardly imagine something this encompassing. Here and there were small groupings of fir trees, but mainly it was those round hills and small valleys. Small and large rock outcroppings completed the terrain. But always, always, the mountains were off in the western distance. They were mesmerizing, hypnotizing. Jack warned me that the distance was very deceiving. They looked so near, maybe a mile or so away, but actually, they were many, many miles off.

"Do you own the mountains too?" I asked excitedly.

"Darlin', only God owns the mountains." But he winked at me so I wasn't really sure.

"Jack, I want to get *close* to the mountains. Get up *in* the mountains. *Feel* the rocks. Be in awe of their mightiness," I chattered excitedly. I couldn't help myself. Coming from the flat Midwest, this view was amazing.

He could see that I was fascinated by the mountains. "Beth, I'll take you to the mountains after I teach you to ride and you're comfortable on a horse. For long rides," he added.

That thought was daunting, but it wasn't nearly enough to curb my excitement.

After one more gate and at the top of another round hill, in the far distance, I could finally see a large stand of trees and some buildings.

"Here we are," Jack said as I studied the landscape ahead of us. The closer we got, the better I could see two houses, one large and one smaller, along with several other buildings and barns. It was a large homestead area, divided here and there by a stand of pines or a row of bushes.

As if he could read my thoughts, which I so often believed he could, Jack said, "We use a couple of jeeps to get around between the buildings. And we have several trucks to take us out on the ranch in a hurry. But most of the cattle work is done on horseback. Right now, we have about thirty horses and a thousand head of cattle."

It was *too much* for me to take in all at once. I didn't want to ask—I was too polite—but I thought Jack *must* have been rich. My mind flitted back to the conversation about the long-distance phone calls, all the flights back and forth between Chicago and Montana, and the clothing he bought for me in Bozeman. And how he was known at the hotel and Western store.

The larger of the two houses was built like a lodge, or what I thought a lodge should look like. Constructed in the log cabin style, but so much larger and grander. Massive logs spanned the front and framed its large windows. It was a two-story house, with wings on either side, each complete with its own peaked roof. A stone foundation supported the entire structure, with a half-dozen steps leading up to the sprawling front entrance. The house was huge, hulking and imposing. Besides feeling simply dwarfed by it, it didn't *seem* friendly or warm. Reflecting on it later, I attributed that feeling to the lack of flowers and any sort of softness surrounding the structure.

The smaller house was of a similar style but was not constructed of logs—more traditionally sided in rough lumber planks, but still impressive. And definitely more welcoming.

As the truck pulled up, a small pack of dogs came bounding down the driveway. Behind the yapping canines, two men came out of one of the barns to join the welcoming party. One was leading a light-colored horse by a halter. The other was in a wheelchair.

"There's Dad and Glenn," Jack indicated.

Which was which? I wondered. He never mentioned that his dad was in a wheelchair. Was that him? How did that happen? Questions raced through my mind.

I tried not to be nervous, but here I was, a stranger, already married into this family. And, it appeared, a very wealthy family. Jack never told me the *extent* of the ranch or the cattle operation or any of this. I didn't know I'd married one of the Cartwrights and moved to the Ponderosa!

I climbed out of the truck as the two men approached us. The man in the wheelchair greeted Jack with a handshake, and then he turned to me.

"Well, Jackson, she's even prettier than you described. Elizabeth, welcome to Montana and the Juddson Ranch. I'm hoping you'll let me stand in for the father you never had, and I sincerely wish that you'll be happy here amongst us cattle folks."

I was stunned by the remark about my father. Before I could react, he took my hand and pulled me into an awkward hug from the wheelchair. I could feel the warmth in his embrace, not just physically but possibly emotionally as well. Could that be?

"Thank you, sir," I stammered, trying not to let *any* of my emotions get the better of me.

"Call me JT," he boomed. "Stands for John Thomas, but everyone calls me JT. I'd be honored if you would too."

He was a big man. Even in the wheelchair, I could tell he was tall. I could see the resemblance between father and son immediately. They were both tall and firmly built, and Jack also had his father's eyes—that same unusual shade of blue, a difficult color to describe. But where Jack's eyes were full of fire and sparks and could cast a piercing stare that could freeze or melt, his father's eyes were older, wiser. I wanted to like him immediately and sensed he imagined the same, but still there was a presence about him I couldn't quite grasp.

"And this old guy is Glenn 'Running Bear' Allister," Jack introduced the other man. "We couldn't run the place without Glenn," he added.

"Elizabeth, it's a pleasure to meet you at last. Since Christmas, *you* are all Jack has talked about. We thought he'd surely been under some kind of spell, but you don't *appear* to be a witch." Glenn winked and made a strange gesture with his hand.

"He's warding off the 'evil eye' and any black magic you might be casting," Jack sarcastically explained. "Sleeping Bear, being part Indian, believes in sorcery, you know."

"Wait, I thought you called him 'Running Bear,'" I said, confused.

"Elizabeth, my name is 'Standing Bear' but this knucklehead you married can't keep it straight," Glenn bantered.

I found out later that Glenn was teased quite a bit with the "adjective" accompanying "Bear." Running Bear, Sleeping Bear, Sitting Bear; they called him just about anything other than Standing Bear. But he pretty much ignored them all and took the kidding in extremely good nature. Fifteen years younger than JT but not quite fifteen years older than Jack, Glenn had been his mentor, older brother, honorary uncle, and partner in crime. The men were close; you could tell not only from the joking, but also from the silent, meaningful looks shared between them.

"And this little lady is Buttercup," Glenn said, rubbing the nose of the horse he was holding.

Not knowing much at all about horses, she didn't look so *little* to me. But she had beautiful coloring, dark cream and light tan—hence her name, I guessed. And her ears twitched when Glenn said her name. Jack asked Glenn when he had gotten Buttercup.

"Just last week," he told him.

"Darlin', Buttercup will be your horse. We've been looking for a gentle mare for you and one that's not too big." He must have seen the panic in my eyes, because he said, "Oh, it'll take some time to get to know each other."

"Maybe Elizabeth would like to go riding now? Glenn and one of the hands can get the truck unloaded," JT suggested.

"Dad, I think Beth would like to see her house. Besides, we've been on the road and living out of duffel bags for more than a week. There will be plenty of time for her to get acquainted with Buttercup. And we haven't had any lunch yet." Jack sounded...what? Almost *testy* when he replied to JT.

But I was relieved. I did reach out to pet Buttercup, but she snuffled and it startled me. Even for a *small* horse, she looked quite big to me.

Jack and I headed over to the "little" house while Glenn headed to the barn and JT wheeled his chair toward the ramp to the "big" house's porch. JT hollered out that we'd find some lunch fixings in the refrigerator.

~~~~~~

As Glenn led Buttercup to the barn, he saw a movement out of the corner of his eye. Handing the bridle off to a ranch hand, Glenn quickly made his way to the edge of the building just in time to see Cathy sneaking off toward the pines. "She's gonna be nothing but trouble," he mumbled to himself.

~~~~~~

The "little" house, as they called it, was the original house, Jack explained, where his grandmother and grandfather had lived and raised their children. Over the years, it had been added on to and rooms had been expanded. Then, after the "big" house was built, the little house had been remodeled and refurbished so that not much of the original house remained. However, the large stone fireplace in the living room was unchanged from the original version. The little house had been called the "guest cottage" until a few months ago when it became known that Jack was getting married. Little did I know that not only had the house been renamed, but also redecorated to suit the newlyweds. The kitchen had been updated by adding a dishwasher, and a huge king-sized bed had been purchased for the master bedroom.

Jack winked at me, put his arm around me, and said he had other plans for lunch. At the foot of the steps to the little house, he stopped and turned me toward him. "Well, Mrs. Juddson, we're gonna start this out right." And with that, he scooped me up in his arms and carried me up the three stairs, across the porch, and over the threshold into our house. Setting me down in the middle of the living room, he didn't release me. He pulled me close and kissed me deeply for many moments. "Beth, I hope you'll be happy here. I love you, darlin', and I'm so happy you are finally here." He took my hand and led me upstairs to the new king-sized bed he said just *had* to be "broken in."

Later in the afternoon, we left the bedroom to find something to eat. Someone had thoughtfully stocked the fridge with a couple of bottles of champagne, and Jack opened one while I rummaged through the cabinets trying to find glasses. I wanted to see the entire house, so, carrying our champagne, Jack gave me a guided tour. In the hallway off the living room was a huge wooden cabinet; when I tried to open it, I found that it was locked. I asked Jack about this and he told me, "Darlin', that's the gun closet. Best to keep it locked."

Jack stretched on his toes to reach the top of the cabinet, fumbling around until he found a key. Unlocking the doors, he opened the cabinet. I drew back. There must have been a dozen shotguns or rifles—I didn't know one from the other—lined up in the rack slots. I had gotten used to the cowboy boots and the hat, but I never anticipated there would be guns.

"Darlin', we all carry a gun on the ranch," he explained, once again reading my thoughts. "You never know when you might need one. To protect the herd, you might have to shoot a mountain lion or a wolf."

I saw for myself the next day that they did indeed wear gun belts just like you'd see in a John Wayne movie. And I found out later that Jack had a pistol packed in his duffel bag during our entire trip to Montana.

Downstairs, in addition to the modern kitchen and huge living room with the old stone fireplace, there was a den and a dining room. The kitchen was large enough for a small table and I thought we'd have most meals there—breakfast for sure. There was a small half bath downstairs, off the kitchen. Upstairs there was the master bedroom suite, with its own bathroom, as well as two other bedrooms that shared another full bath.

"It's a lot of room for just the two of us," I commented.

"Room for babies," he said with a wink.

We had talked about having children, *of course*. I knew he wanted several. And *if* I could even get pregnant, I wanted kids too, but not yet. I'd been on the pill since before Christmas and still would be for the immediate future, thanks to the six-month supply I got before I left the university. I needed time to adjust to Jack, to Montana, and to this way of life. I also wanted to teach for a few years before I had any babies. Not unreasonable, I thought. But I did feel a twinge of guilt that I hadn't shared the tipped uterus situation with Jack.

~~~~~~

Jack told me we'd be expected for dinner up at the "big" house at seven p.m. with *cocktails* before.

I started to ask, but with that sense of his, he answered, "We don't 'dress' for dinner here, darlin'. Jeans and boots are fine."

~~~~~~

Later, as we walked the short distance between the houses, I tried to imagine Jack growing up in that enormous house and JT now living there all by himself, since Jack and I would spend most of our time in the smaller house.

Walking up the wide steps to the front door, I again sensed the brooding presence of the dark-wooded dwelling. Scolding myself, I shook it off and put a smile on my face. *This is not Manderley and I'm not Rebecca and there is no other Mrs. Juddson, other than Jack's mother.*

But the inside was just as overwhelming as the outside. The front door entered directly into the living room. There was a massive stone fireplace that dominated one wall. Like the outside of the house, the inside walls were made of logs. In addition, round beams—stained, varnished, and complete with original knotty nubs—crossed the ceiling.

As I stared at the dark and heavy logs over my head, JT rolled his chair close to me and said, "Don't worry, Elizabeth.

They won't fall on you. Those logs have been up there for over three decades and have survived numerous thunderstorms, several blizzards, and even an earthquake or two."

"Sounds like I have a lot to look forward to...weather-wise," I murmured.

The living room, spanning the entire front middle section of the building, was a large open space with a high ceiling. Looking up, I could see hallways on each side that led off into the upper wings. Log beams featured prominently in the upper level as well.

Someone must have cut down a forest to build this place.

Glenn handed me the beer I shyly agreed to and then JT hustled me onto a tour of the "lodge," as I thought of it.

JT rolled his chair toward the formal dining room. "It seats *fourteen*," he bragged.

And comfortably, I could see. Beyond the dining room was an extremely large kitchen. With a terracotta floor and the latest "harvest-gold" appliances, it was surprisingly southwestern. In addition to the very large refrigerator, there was a walk-in pantry. Copper-bottomed pots and pans hung from hooks over what looked like a large brick oven in the center of the room. *Is that really an indoor barbeque pit?* I stepped closer to get a better look. There was a heavy metal grate covering a bed of ashes. *Yep, big enough to grill a small cow.*

A laundry room finished off the center floor plan.

JT boasted that each upper wing had three bedrooms and some shared bathrooms. *Six bedrooms!* I did get to poke my head into the lower-wing areas, which held an office, a den, a library, and a TV room. And a couple more bathrooms. *Who cleans all of this?*

We made our way back to the living room with its floor-to-ceiling windows. Dark, heavy curtains framed the windows. What little daylight filtered in could never compete with the darkness of the paneling and beams above.

It was a very *masculine* home: oversized dark leather couches and armchairs; rusted ranch tools scattered here and there; and a couple of antlered animal heads in prominent positions hung on the walls. The lack of warmth was overwhelming. *Is it merely the absence of any feminine touches? Or something else?*

Jack had told me that his mother died when he was only six. He didn't talk much about her, but he must have had *some* memories of her. I hadn't pressed him on the subject since I knew firsthand the ache of not having a parent, but I hoped in time he would open up to me about her.

"How was the trip out, Elizabeth?" JT asked. "This is your first time to Montana, is it not? What do you think of our Big Sky state?"

"It's emptier than I imagined," I told him honestly.

"Wide open spaces to ride Buttercup," he said defensively.

"Yes, that will be...fun to do," I replied lamely. *I hope the riding lessons don't start immediately.*

"You'll get used to ranch life, Elizabeth. It's the greatest way to live."

"I'm hoping to get a teaching job this fall," I told him, not exactly dismissing "ranch life" but indicating there were other ways of life.

JT turned to Jack, and a look passed between them that I couldn't comprehend.

After I answered a few more awkward questions, Jack steered the conversation back to the ranch. The four of us were clustered at one end of the gigantic table for fourteen. I studied what I could of the room. A big sideboard took up half of one wall. Large old china plates, with a pattern I'd have to look at more closely later, adorned the walls like family portraits. No windows because the wings backed up to this room. Fortunately, however, no animal heads stared down accusingly while we ate.

I daydreamed and enjoyed the food and wine, while the men talked about moving this herd or that herd to this range or that range; summer hay supplies; heifers and steers, cows and bulls, and calves. When the conversation moved on to the horses or ranch hands, I tried to pay attention, but it was like a language all their own. Between the wine and being road-weary, I only followed bits and pieces and wished for the evening to end.

Finally, dessert and coffee were served. I discovered during dinner that not only did the big house have a cook, but the ranch also employed several other domestics. There were ten or so ranch hands at any given time working the cattle, cutting and baling hay, or tending the horses. Now I could understand why it would have been hard for JT to come east for the wedding, between the confinement of his wheelchair and the fact that he was running a huge cattle operation. And, totally unbeknownst me to, I'd married into it.

~~~~~~

Before Jack drifted off to sleep, he once again congratulated himself on a mission accomplished. He had found Beth, courted her, *and* gotten her to marry him. And now she was here on the ranch, sleeping next to him. All that was left was getting her pregnant. *That* should be fun. He chuckled to himself. As shy as she was in the beginning, she was quickly becoming an active sex partner. He so enjoyed making love to her, hearing her sighs and soft moans, knowing he was the one who opened her up to the pleasures of sex.

He couldn't stop himself from once again comparing Beth to Cathy. Day and night. Heaven and hell...*hath no fury*, he thought. But he didn't want to dwell on Cathy right now. She hadn't taken *no* for an answer at all. It was barely a week after she had stomped off from the rock and she had showed up at the ranch as if nothing had changed. He didn't want to make a scene in front of the ranch hands, so he acted like he was too busy to even talk to her. He wanted to tell her to just stay off the ranch and not come around anymore. But she *was* a neighbor and she *had* been visiting the ranch for years. He just didn't think the ruckus over him marrying Beth was over for Cathy. He needed to get Glenn off by himself tomorrow to find out what, if anything, she'd been up to.

CHAPTER 14

The next morning, I had planned to make breakfast for my cowboy husband, but he was gone when I finally woke up. He left a note that said he would get breakfast at the big house, but he'd be back for lunch, after which we would go riding.

Great—riding lessons on my first day here.

I straightened the bed covers and then took a quick shower. Jack had thoughtfully brought up the bag of clothes from Donnelly's. Pulling on a T-shirt and one of the new pairs of jeans, I alternated between high-stepping and duck-walking, trying to loosen the fabric. *If the horse ride didn't chafe my thighs, this stiff denim surely will.* Grabbing my hat, I hurried downstairs.

Someone had unloaded the truck and all my boxes were neatly stacked in one of the spare bedrooms. I started opening boxes and carrying clothes to our bedroom, where I appropriated dresser drawers and closet space. Mom's stuff would have to wait; I pushed the metal lockbox to the back of the closet. The books were another problem.

Close to noon, I headed to the kitchen to see about lunch. I was contemplating what Jack might like to eat when I looked out the window and saw him heading to the house in one of the jeeps. Goodness me, he was a handsome man. That black hair curling on his neck under his hat. I watched him park and slide out. So tall and strong. I didn't think he could see me from that angle through the screen, but Jack looked right where I was standing and grinned that devilish leer. The way he was unbuckling his gun belt, I knew exactly what *he* wanted for lunch.

~~~~~~

In the afternoon, as promised, I had my first riding lesson on Buttercup. Jack kept telling me that Buttercup was small, as horses go, and I could see that she *was* smaller in comparison to, say, *his* horse. But still, straddling Buttercup's mammoth girth stretched muscles that I didn't know I had. You'd think after all the sex I'd had recently, I'd be more flexible, but I still was quite uncomfortable with my inner thighs so extended.

We only rode for an hour or so, mostly around the corral at first, then around the homestead. I wasn't sure I would be able to stand when I finally dismounted, but, although wobbly, thank goodness my legs held me up. What kind of a cowboy's wife would I be if my legs gave out after my very first short ride?

~~~~~~

Well, at least she hasn't fallen off yet, Jack thought. Beth did look kind of cute perched on Buttercup, with a death grip on the saddle horn. He chuckled to himself, remembering her arguing last night that she didn't need to learn how to ride a horse.

"Beth," he'd said, "out here everyone needs to know how to ride."

"But why can't I just learn how to drive a jeep or an ATV?"

"Well, for one thing horses don't need gas, and for another, horses don't get flat tires. All it takes is one good puncture from a set of elk or deer antlers, and you'd be stuck."

He could see her discarding the image of changing a flat on a jeep or ATV, and he knew she'd come riding the next day. And dang, if she didn't look the part in her new "cowgirl" clothes, as she called them. He loved watching her backside bounce on the saddle. She would sure be sore later. And then he smiled again, thinking how he would soothe those aches.

~~~~~~

Thank goodness that Jack had begged off dinner at the big house so we could have dinner alone. He told me his dad was upset at first, but then Glenn reminded JT we were newlyweds. And when Jack gave me a sexy wink, I knew what *we* were having for dessert.

~~~~~~

What Jack *didn't* tell Beth was that Glenn also told his dad, "JT, you're probably too old to remember what that was like, being honeymooners. We need to give Jack and Elizabeth some alone time. You want that grandson, don't you?" As if he needed more reminding that getting Beth knocked up was his top priority.

~~~~~~

On my first day of riding, I was so focused on all of Jack's instructions: hold on with your legs; keep your heels down; don't grab the saddle horn. That last one was so very tempting. But the next day, I didn't have to *think* so much about staying on Buttercup. I can't say I was getting *used* to riding, but—even though my thighs were still protesting the stretch to fit around Buttercup—I could at least start to enjoy the scenery.

I wanted to know how JT had ended up in the wheelchair but didn't know exactly how to approach the subject with Jack. I didn't want to be rude or pry. But I *was* very curious. I just hadn't found the right moment to bring it up.

Jack and I rode a bit farther from the ranch boundary and, after a brief gallop (my first!) between two of those numerous hilly mounds, we walked the horses for a stretch.

"Jack, how long has your dad been in the wheelchair?" I asked shyly.

Jack was quiet for so long that I wondered if he had heard me. Finally, he said, "It's been about ten years now." It was almost like he had needed the time to do the math.

"Was he in an accident?"

"Yes."

He didn't offer any further explanation. His jaw was clenched, and the warm sparkle in his eyes had turned to frosty ice.

"Must be hard for him," I mumbled, but I didn't think he heard me.

~~~~~~

Jack came to the little house around mid-morning later that first week. I was still unpacking boxes, but I came downstairs when I heard him come in. I had dressed for the day in the usual ranch outfit, jeans and a T-shirt, but I was wearing my sneakers, which was my preference around the house.

"Beth, where are your boots?" he asked.

"Jack, they're in the mudroom where they belong. They're boots." I had only been wearing them to ride Buttercup.

"Why aren't you wearing them?"

"Well," I hemmed, "they are hot and not very comfortable.

Stiff. And noisy. I'm *clumping* around the house on these wood floors."

"They're not broken in yet. You have to wear 'em to make 'em more comfortable. You should be wearing 'em, or they'll never get broken in."

"How long does that take?" I asked in a petulant tone.

"There's no exact time schedule," Jack laughed. "The more you wear 'em, the more comfortable they'll be."

Just like us. Eventually.

~~~~~~

I wasn't used to riding, and of course I was sore after the second day. When I complained a little about getting back on a horse the third day and wondered if we could take one of the pickup trucks instead, he told me, "'You can see what *man* made from the seat of an automobile, but the best way to see what *God* made is from the back of a horse.' That's what Charlie Russell says, anyway."

"Who's Charlie Russell? Is he a friend of yours? Will I get to meet him?"

Jack burst out laughing. "Oh, darlin', Charlie Russell is about the most famous cowboy painter ever." He chuckled. "His paintings are legend around here. And he didn't just paint cowboys, but Indians and landscapes too. Why, there's a famous mural of his over in the state capitol building. In Helena," he reminded me. "I'll take you there one day and show you. Russell was able to capture on canvas our way of life, out here in the West," he said proudly.

~~~~~~

Just as I had shown him my world back in the college town, Jack took me riding almost every afternoon and showed me the raw beauty of Montana. There were no trails where we rode. It was just as he had described it to me before we were married. The wide-open range. Big Sky Country! In my mind, it was much hillier than "open range" conjures. To me, it looked like God had taken a giant ice cream scoop and dropped round mounds hither and yon. No pattern; some close, some farther apart. Most so tall that you couldn't see over one to the next. This was what created these sheltered valleys. Occasionally we would see one of the herds of cattle, spread out in the distance. When I asked him if the cattle just meandered, he smiled and told me that several times over the summer they had cattle drives to move the herds to different areas. Left on their own, cattle would just overgraze an area.

What I didn't know was that these riding lessons were more than time spent together out of Jack's busy day. They were also opportunities for Jack to check on the herds, assess grazing areas, check fences, and look over the hay storage buildings.

On one of our rides, we came upon a deer carcass. It was mostly bones, some antlers, and a few tufts of hide, so I couldn't tell what it had been, but Jack pointed out the outline of a deer in the skeletal remains.

"Mountain lion probably got it," he told me in a matter-of-fact tone.

I shivered, thinking of the helpless deer being viciously torn apart. But a thought never crossed my mind about the hungry cougar.

CHAPTER 15

Jack and I settled into a pattern over the next couple of weeks. Although I thought we'd have breakfast together, most days he had an early breakfast at the big house with JT and Glenn. I was invited as well, but most mornings I didn't make it up in time. Then, around lunchtime, he would show up at the little house and we would have lunch or make love. Some days we did both.

One morning, I managed to get up early enough to have breakfast with the men. I let myself into the big house and, as I was heading toward the dining room, I heard JT ask, "Jackson, when are you going to get that filly bred?"

I figured they were talking about a horse. I heard Jack say something like, "As soon as I can wean her off…" His voice dropped just then so I couldn't hear what he said. It sounded like he said "wean her off of Bill." But that didn't make any sense to me. Did they really name a mare "Bill"? Maybe it was short for Wilhelmina, I thought, smiling to myself. Could you breed a horse that had just been weaned? Seemed too early to me, but what did I know about any of this?

My boots clicked on the floor outside the dining room

and I heard Glenn, facing the entrance to the room, clear his throat. "Good *afternoon*, Elizabeth," he teased me. They had already finished eating and were lingering over their coffee. I knew the men got up while it was still dark, did some chores, and then had breakfast. I had been trying to get up early so that I could at least see Jack for a few minutes in the morning. But it had been a struggle for me.

"Good *morning*, 'Funny Bear,'" I countered, and both JT and Jack laughed.

I fixed myself a plate from the sideboard and the men stood as I seated myself. The long-time cook, Sarah, came in just then with a fresh pot of coffee to see if the men needed anything else. By the time she left, the conversation had moved on to wheat prices and the new Alaskan pipeline that had just been authorized.

~~~~~~

I developed a routine in my first few weeks at the ranch. In the mornings, I would do some housework around the little house. I spent time organizing the kitchen to suit me. I worked on closets and drawers. All of that made me feel that it was *my* house too. Then, in the afternoons, I would go riding with Jack. After our ride, I would go back to the little house and read or write a letter to Lucy.

Once or twice, Jack was too busy in the afternoon to take me riding, and I was not allowed to go out by myself. I didn't protest when Jack made this rule, because I was not sure I knew my way around well enough anyway. We'd go in a different direction every day. On one of these non-riding afternoons, I found out that the domestic help working in the big house took care of the little house as well. I came upon Ruby, Sarah's daughter, cleaning the upstairs bathrooms. I always made the bed and I had been doing the laundry, but Ruby insisted that she could do the laundry.

We'd been on the ranch now for about a month. Although the surrounding landscape was breathtakingly beautiful, there was a remoteness to the ranch that was sometimes unsettling. As if Jack could read my thoughts, he announced on one Thursday that we would be "going to town" on Saturday.

"All the way to Bozeman?" I asked him.

"No, there's a smaller town between here and there that we go to most weekends."

This was news to me, as *most* weekends Jack and I had stayed on the ranch. But I got caught up in the excitement of going somewhere new, and when Saturday morning arrived, I almost beat Jack out of bed.

~~~~~~

A small convoy headed into town: pickup trucks loaded with ranch hands, a jeep driven by Glenn with JT riding shotgun and his wheelchair in the back, and a second jeep carrying Jack and me. Jack had explained that it would take a good half-hour to get there. It actually took longer because of all the gates, but eventually we came to some houses on the outskirts and then the town itself. Besides two churches, three gas stations, and a tavern, there was a general store that carried cattle and horse feed as well as some basic clothing and food items. There was a larger grocery store with more selections, an old-fashioned drug store, a barber shop, a bowling alley, a movie theater, and a doctor's office. There were a few sad-looking shops: women's clothing, a jewelry store, and a five-and-dime. There was a florist/gift/Western Union store and, of course, the local gossip hub, the Busy Bee Café.

However, the biggest surprise of all was the name of the town: Juddson. I looked at Jack and started to say something, but the look on his face stopped me. Walking on the sidewalk in front of Juddson's General Store was a short, blonde woman, waving and smiling widely at Jack. Glenn pulled into one of the diagonal parking places in front of the store, as did the ranch hands. I thought at first that Jack was going to keep right on going, past the store, down the block, but at the last possible second, he swung the jeep into a spot next to one of the pickup trucks.

"Well, hiya, Judd," the blonde woman hollered.

Jack nodded and said, "Cathy."

"I've been wondering when you'd bring Elizabeth to town so we could finally meet her," she cooed.

Startled that she knew my name, I turned to Jack, but he was tangled up with the ranch hands exiting the truck and I couldn't see his face. I came up to the sidewalk from the other side of the jeep, and Cathy introduced herself.

"Hi Elizabeth, I'm Cathy Wimberly from the Sweetwater Ranch. Welcome to Montana." She stuck out her hand, and when I reciprocated, she pumped my hand furiously with a cowgirl's grip. "I'm so happy to finally meet you. Those boys have kept you hidden away far too long." She winked at Jack who, by this time, stood alongside JT in his chair.

Cathy was a petite, vivacious, curly-headed blonde with the greenest eyes. Although short, her body was proportionately attractive, and I could see the ranch hands eyeing her figure appreciatively. I didn't know where she fit into Jack's life, so I was withholding judgment until I learned more. For the time being, I couldn't help but like her. Cathy was the first female my age I'd met in Montana.

"First visit to town?" she asked.

"Yes," I told her, but I had a feeling she already knew this.

"So, *however* did Jack *find* you?" she asked pointedly.

I told her that we met in Illinois by chance.

"Oh, I doubt it was *by chance*," she countered. It seemed she was going to say more, but a piercing look from Jack cut her short. There was an awkward pause, and then JT and Glenn started to move toward the door of the store. Jack took my elbow to move me along.

"I hope we'll see more of you," I said sincerely. Missing Lucy, I wondered if Cathy might fill the girlfriend void.

"Oh sure, I'll be around," she replied. "I get over to your place every now and then." She winked at Jack, *again*, and said, "See ya, Judd," although it sounded more like "See ya, *stud*" to me. And with a toss of blonde hair, she headed toward a truck parked down the block.

The men walked into the store while Jack and I headed down the block in the opposite direction from Cathy. I started to ask Jack about Cathy but we hadn't made it halfway down the block before he was introducing me to someone else. *I guess if you have a town named after you, most folks know you.*

~~~~~~

After lunch at the Busy Bee, Jack showed me more of the town. Past the Busy Bee, heading out of town in the opposite direction, there was a bank, a funeral home, and, surprisingly, a library.

I tugged Jack's sleeve toward the library entrance. "I want to see if they have any new books," I told him. I also wanted a list of schools in the area so I could start applying for a job—but I didn't tell him this.

It might have been begrudgingly, I wasn't sure, but he opened the door to the library and we went in. The library was small by any standard; one room with shelves on each wall. The "new book" section was barely a full shelf of books. Mostly last year's bestsellers: *Love Story* and *The French Lieutenant's Woman*, both of which I'd already read, as well as a few others. I was hoping to get Herman Wouk's new book, *The*

Winds of War. Disappointing.

The librarian was a young girl, probably still in high school. "Do you have a Montana School Directory?" I inquired.

She looked at me like I spoke in Russian and then looked at Jack. She blushed all the way to her hairline.

"It's okay, honey," he soothed. "We don't need it now."

I was about to protest that, *yes*, we did need it *now*. It was summer and I needed to send out résumés. But Jack gave me a look that said, *"Don't argue,"* tipped his hat at the young librarian, and nudged me out the door. *This conversation is not over.*

Leaving the library and continuing down the block, the tour was completed as we passed the City Hall/Police/Fire Department, all housed in one small building, and a car dealership, which mostly had jeeps and pickup trucks. Peeking down the side streets, I could see a small school building a block over.

"What about that school?" I asked Jack.

"It was an elementary school but closed several years ago."

At the very edge of town, there was a hardware store with a lumber yard on the side.

I still couldn't believe the town bore their name, but Jack was either bashfully reserved or totally immune to the novelty of a town named after him.

"So, how did there come to be a town with your family name?" I finally had to ask.

At first, he didn't say anything. "Well, Beth, one of my grandfather's brothers started the town. Mainly out of necessity for the feed and general store items. That was the first and only building for a long time. And then, as time went on, the rest of the town just grew around the store," he explained. "It's no big deal, Beth," he told me, his tone indicating the topic was closed.

As I was still getting used to the "Cartwright" lifestyle, I realized I'd just have to add having a small town named after your family to the list. I couldn't wait to write Lucy and tell her.

~~~~~~

While showing Beth around Juddson, Jack was still trying to work out in his mind what Cathy was up to. Was she trying to cause trouble? She certainly had a lot of experience doing just that. Knowing her as he did, he wouldn't put anything past her. He knew she still wanted him. Mostly to fuck her. And he figured the fury wasn't over.

~~~~~~

On the way back to the ranch, I tried to question Jack about Cathy. Riding in the open jeep, however, was not conducive to conversation. When we got back to the ranch, I launched into a thorough interrogation.

"So, how long have you known Cathy?" was my first question.

"Forever, it seems. The Wimberlys are neighbors," he told me, then added, "If you can count Sweetwater Ranch being ten miles away as 'neighbors.'"

"Did you date Cathy?" I asked.

"Beth, we practically grew up together. She's like a sister to me," Jack stated.

"She doesn't act very *sisterly*," I pointed out.

"Yeah, we went out a couple of times in high school. Nothing serious."

I was curious if he'd slept with her, but I didn't know how to ask and I wasn't sure if I really wanted to know the answer.

~~~~~~

Jack felt bad lying to Beth about Cathy. But, really, what could he tell her? He already had one woman royally pissed at him; he was smart enough to know he didn't need a second one.

One time, when he and Beth were out riding, Jack spotted another rider in the distance. Beth was too focused on keeping her heels down and her hands off the horn to notice, but it was clear to Jack who the rider was. Cathy angled away before they came too close, but Jack would recognize her from any distance.

Just last week, Jack had finally been able to corner Glenn and ask him how Cathy had been acting since he broke the news to her.

"Ominously quiet," Glenn told him. "She still comes by the ranch from time to time, appears to be looking for you, but trying not to be obvious about it. More or less like she's always done."

Jack was thinking that over when Glenn added, "But I have to tell you, don't turn your back on her. You know how crazy she can be, so there's no telling what she might do. Just try not to encourage her. And for godsakes, don't fuck her."

Talk about a crapload of advice. Don't turn my back on her, don't encourage her, and don't fuck her. Great. "Any other sage advice, WiseAss Bear?" Jack sarcastically asked Glenn.

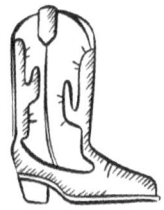

CHAPTER 16

I had too much time on my hands. Every day, I had several hours to try and fill. I missed Lucy. I missed swimming. I missed museums and art galleries. I missed a good library.

The little house was finally organized the way I wanted. Jack didn't appear to care, as he spent more time at the big house than in *our* house. He ate most of his meals there. Which was not how I envisioned our married life would be. I had fantasies of cooking and baking for him, but all that was taken care of by Sarah.

To pass the time, I would walk about the homestead, exploring the many buildings and barns. One time, I was coming around the corner of the shop building where the men worked on the pickup trucks and the farm machinery. One of the younger men was talking about his girlfriend.

"Man, she has a sweet ass. Have you seen it as she's riding off on the dun?"

"Jack'd take you apart if he heard you talking like that. And *then* he'd fire you."

I knew that Jack would not tolerate any of the hands abusing women, but this seemed pretty mild to me. After all, men will be men, as my mother used to say. "Men are never too old to look, Elizabeth," she would say. "And when they stop looking, honey, they're dead."

"I heard JT tell Glenn that he expects a passel of 'young'uns' over the next few years. With the record number of calves born this past spring, and now Jack being married, he's hoping their luck is finally on the upswing. Jack's wife is strictly 'hands-off.' But you could have Jack's leftovers," he said with a snicker.

"Ah shit, *everybody's* had a piece of *that* pie. Cathy's nothing but..." and his voice dropped so I didn't catch the last part.

With a start, I realized they were talking about *me*. A passel of "young'uns"? And wait—Jack's "leftovers"? Cathy!

Before I could react, Glenn appeared, and the conversation shifted to replacement parts for the hay baler they were working on. I wasn't sure if Glenn had spotted me on the side of the building, but I crept back the way I'd come. As I hurried over to meet Jack riding in from the range, I thought that I had to find the right time to tell him why I might not be able to have any children. I also wanted to find out exactly how well Jack *knew* Cathy.

~~~~~~

That evening, when we were back in our house after dinner in the Big House once again—and after Jack had drunk at least three beers, if I was counting correctly—I brought up Cathy again.

"Since Cathy lives so close, I was thinking that perhaps she and I could get together socially," I suggested. "I miss Lucy," I went on. "I don't have any girlfriends here. It's *all* men on the ranch. And you're busy every day. Maybe Cathy and I could do some *girl* stuff. I could go riding with her. She's obviously more experienced than I am, so I'd be 'chaperoned.' There's not much to do in Juddson, but maybe Cathy and I could go to Bozeman and have a girl's overnight? You know, shopping, manicures, see a movie?"

I was getting excited about the possibility of getting off the ranch, going to a big city, and being with another woman.

Jack turned his head to look at me, but he was unnaturally quiet.

I still wanted to know their history, so I pressed on. "How long ago did you stop dating her?" *How fresh were those leftovers?* "I didn't get the impression that she's married. Well, I didn't see a ring. But a pretty girl like that must be dating someone, right? Is it someone you know? Maybe all four of us could do something, sometime."

Oh, those blue eyes were sending me a warning. But did I heed it?

"Would it be too uncomfortable having your wife and your ex-girlfriend in the same social situation?" I asked innocently.

Very calmly, Jack turned to me and said, "Beth, I don't want you to socialize *in any way* with Cathy."

"For heaven's sake, why not?" I demanded.

"Because I'm your husband and I told you so," he shouted. "I seem to remember a part of your wedding vows was to *obey*."

I pulled back, shocked at the intensity of his response. I had definitely hit a nerve!

~~~~~~

Jack knew immediately he'd taken the wrong approach with Beth. She rarely argued with him. Mostly she was quite docile. She had acquiesced fairly easily on giving up her car, and there were other times back east when she went along with his decisions without protesting. And of course, here in Montana, where she didn't know the customs or the area, she followed his lead.

But this time...wow! He saw that she *did* have a temper. It took a lot to rile her up, but he sure managed it this time. *Obey*... He cringed.

She got up from the couch and, without saying another word, went up the stairs. But he saw the hurt and anger in her tearful eyes before she left the room.

No sex tonight, he figured.

~~~~~~

I faked being asleep when Jack came up. With my back to his side of the bed, I didn't know if he knew I was pretending. And I didn't really care if he did. He was smart enough not to touch me after telling me to *obey* him.

It took me a long time to *really* fall asleep. I kept hearing Jack's words *shouted* at me, over and over. "Obey!"

Eventually, I did sleep, and Jack was long gone by the time I woke up.

~~~~~~

Although I'd been riding every day for many weeks now, Jack had made it clear that I was never to go out alone.

"If you want to ride, and I'm not here, then one of the ranch hands needs to go with you." He was insistent on this, but I never asked why. It was silly to me. So far Montana seemed so much safer than the big city where I grew up.

It was a beautiful late June morning, and I thought it would be nice to go out on Buttercup. I couldn't find Jack, or even Glenn to ask where Jack was. The young boy in the tack room, who couldn't have been more than twelve or thirteen, didn't look old enough to saddle the horse, much less ride along as my protector. I overrode his protests about having orders to accompany me. I guessed that all the men had those orders. Well. I was not a child. And I was still angry about last night. I could do as I damn well pleased. And fuck *obeying*. I took Buttercup out by myself.

It was a wonderful ride. The mountains looked extra close today—possibly due to the clear, clean air. Heading in that general direction, it was easy to forget the ranch, JT, and even Jack. There was a freedom in being all by myself for the first time since we came to Montana. I wouldn't gallop Buttercup by myself, but we set a nice trot with an occasional fast lope. Looking back over my shoulder to get my bearings, I couldn't see the ranch due to the slight rise we had just crossed. At that moment, Buttercup took a "crow hop" step sideways. I lost a stirrup and then my balance, and down I went with a loud "Umphfft" as I hit the ground, the air knocked out of me. Buttercup startled, then took off at a gallop in the direction from which we had just ridden. The whole thing happened so fast.

I wasn't hurt. Well, my pride was wounded. I had finally fallen off. Jack said that everyone who rides a horse falls off one eventually. I started walking back in the direction of the ranch. Buttercup was long gone. I was hoping she might stop once she got over that rise, but, as I found out later, she did not. She ran flat out, like a horse possessed by demons, all the way back to the ranch. When Jack saw Buttercup flying up the lane, riderless, he took the nearest horse, grabbed a handful of mane, leaped up on its back, and within seconds was galloping off in the direction from which Buttercup had fled.

I had walked for about twenty minutes before I saw a rider galloping toward me. When I saw it was Jack, I was relieved that I wouldn't have to admit to anyone else that I'd fallen off. But when he got closer, oh, those eyes said it all.

He sprung off the horse and took me by both arms. "Are you okay, Beth? My God, when I saw Buttercup without you...

I'd thought the worst. I imagined you lying out here with a broken neck!"

"I'm fine," I assured him. "Except for my pride."

When he could see that I was fine, the look in his eyes changed. His hold on my arm became a vise-like grip. "I've a good mind to take my belt off and give you a good strapping for disobeying me. Didn't I tell you not to go out alone? It's dangerous out here, Beth. There are mountain lions and rattlesnakes. Grizzlies come down from the mountains. You are *never* to be out here alone; do you understand me?" He was shouting at this point.

"Yes," I said meekly. I'd never seen him this angry.

"The next time you disobey me, by God, I swear I'll tan your hide."

And with that, Jack grabbed my arm and tugged me toward the horse. He made a loop with his hands and roughly said, "Get on." He jumped up behind me and reached again for a hunk of mane while securing me to him with his other arm. He urged the horse back in the direction of the homestead. Nothing was said on the way back—or when we got back, for that matter. Glenn asked if I was okay as we went past the barn toward the little house.

"She's fine," Jack growled.

Glenn's eyebrows shot up, but he wisely did not say anything.

Jack slid off the horse and helped me down. "I have work to do," he grumbled and left me at the steps of our house.

~~~~~~

This is just not my day. Jack grumbled to himself as he turned the horse toward the nearest corral. First, JT "ripped him a new one" in front of a few of the hands. It was one thing to get a dressing-down in front of Glenn, but did the old man have to undermine what *very* little authority Jack had over the hands? In spite of the damn chair, JT still ran the ranch with an iron fist. Jack had tried over and over to talk to him about some new ranching ideas he'd learned at the university, but JT just wouldn't budge from his old ways. Still blamed Jack for everything—Beth not getting pregnant soon enough. The hay not getting cut quick enough. The herds not being moved fast enough. And, of course, his ending up in that chair.

And now this incident with Beth. What was she thinking? He told her to *never* go out on her own. What fucking part of *obey* in those vows did she not understand? When he saw Buttercup charging into the yard, his heart about stopped. Jack could only imagine her dead in the prairie. Rattler. Cougar. Maybe even a bear. And when she was fine, what did he do? Threatened her with his belt.

He would never lay a hand on her. He'd fired guys for less. Wouldn't blame her if she was upstairs packing her bags right now. Wanting to get as far away from the Neanderthal as possible. What was he *thinking*?

Out of the corner of his eye, he saw the kid. Damn stupid kid. Well, shit flows downhill, as the expression goes; he made a beeline for him.

~~~~~~

Jack came back much later in the afternoon, long after lunch, his mood no longer dark and angry. *My* anger had disappeared, too, like the wind knocked out of me when I fell off Buttercup. He found me in the den, writing a letter to Lucy.

"I'm sorry I shouted at you, Beth. I was scared. I thought you'd been hurt," he told me as he coaxed me into his arms. "I don't know what I'd do if something happened to you." He buried his head in my neck and just held me.

"I'm sorry too," I confessed. "I shouldn't have taken

Buttercup out alone. But don't blame the stable boy. It's not his fault. I pulled rank."

"Oh, you needn't worry about him. He's gone. I fired him. It's one thing if my wife won't follow orders, but if the men I'm paying can't, then they can work elsewhere."

~~~~~~

I felt bad about the boy. Nothing I said would change Jack's mind about firing him. A few days later, I was out in the barn brushing Buttercup when Glenn came up to me.

"Hi, Elizabeth. Behaving yourself?" he asked pointedly.

"Very funny, *Nosey* Bear," I chided, and Buttercup's ears twitched.

"Elizabeth, I know you are upset about the boy losing his job. But let me tell you something. It's a tough life out here. We have rules. For everyone's protection. The boy should have saddled one of the horses and gone with you. At the very least, he should have found me or Jack and told us you took off by yourself. He learned a valuable lesson. And hopefully you have, too."

I kept grooming Buttercup as I didn't trust myself not to blubber a response. I just nodded.

"She's beautiful, isn't she?"

I didn't know if he was talking to me about Buttercup or to Buttercup about me, but when I looked up to gauge his expression, he was leaving the barn.

CHAPTER 17

Two weeks later, we had a visitor to the ranch: Cathy Wimberly from the Sweetwater Ranch, as she had introduced herself the day I met her in Juddson.

From the kitchen window, where I was cleaning up the lunch dishes, I watched her ride into the ranch. She was on a big horse, not a small one like Buttercup, and she headed straight for Jack. I couldn't hear them, of course, but Cathy leaned over the neck of her horse, carrying on an intense conversation. *And to give him a peek down her blouse.*

Jack threw back his head and laughed, and the little green fiend of jealousy rose in me. Still not sure about their past, and although I knew that Jack loved me, Cathy was many things I wasn't. She was extremely comfortable on her horse; something I had not mastered yet. She was perky and outgoing; I was shy and more of an introvert. Cathy had a great body, petite but proportionately curvaceous, and she exuded a sex appeal that was impossible to ignore.

Why didn't he marry her? Why me? I knew nothing about horses or ranches. For Cathy, this was second nature. Jack did tell me that she had practically grown up on his ranch.

Someone like her would be a better fit than a "city girl" like me, right? Beyond the jealousy, I could feel the old insecurities worming their way into my new life.

Upon seeing this ranch, its size, all the herds, and then the town with the same name, I was beginning to understand the wealth and *power* and influence that the Juddsons held in this area. *That I had married into.*

So why hadn't Jack married someone local? Why had he come all the way to the Midwest to find a wife? I would imagine there were plenty of local girls who'd be more than willing to marry this rugged cowboy. I'd bet he'd been pursued by more than one "gold-digger." In the movies, didn't the rancher's son usually marry the cowgirl next door, expanding the ranch and building a dynasty? So that would be Cathy, right?

Funny how I knew nothing of all this wealth when I fell in love with him and agreed to marry him. *But still, why me?*

~~~~~

In mid-July, Jack told me he was going with the men to "move the herd." This apparently was done several times over the summer, and the previous times this season had been supervised by Glenn. Jack had not taken "his turn." It involved a night or two away from the ranch and, although it would be our first time apart since we'd been married, he insisted that it was time for him to quit shirking this duty. We made crazy passionate love the night before he was to leave, and I slept so soundly that I didn't hear him leave in the morning. The man amazed me with how he could wake up before dawn without an alarm clock.

I found a note downstairs telling me to behave myself. Ever since I went riding alone, that had a particular meaning.

Around midday, my period started, and I wondered if he had my menstrual cycle calendar in his head. Perfect timing to be away from me for a day or two. During previous times of the month, we had at least kissed and cuddled. One time, I had been exceptionally bold and successfully satisfied him with my hand. Although he said he greatly enjoyed it, he thought it was too one-sided and not fair to me, though I was pretty proud of myself for *pulling* that off.

In the afternoon, I decided a walk around the property would kill some time before dinner alone with JT in the big house. There was a small cemetery on the edge of the property that I'd seen while riding but had never had the time to properly explore. The graveyard was tucked away behind some of the outer buildings, nestled in a small grove of pines. Looking at the deteriorating headstones, I recognized the names of Jack's grandparents. A few stones over, I spotted Jack's mother, Ida Mae. Studying her headstone and quickly doing the math, I realized she was only thirty-four when she died. But more puzzling were the smaller graves beside her. I counted five. Good Lord, she had lost five babies! One of the tiny graves had just one date on it, which coincided with the date of Ida Mae's death. She had died in childbirth. I thought again about how I could get Jack to talk about her. And I still had not found out how JT had ended up in that wheelchair. *So many secrets here.*

~~~~~~

When Jack returned from moving the cattle a few days later, all he did for the next two weeks was work. Some nights he went back out after dinner, and even though I tried to stay awake, I'd fall asleep holding the book I was reading, with the bedroom lights on, before he came back to the little house. When I'd wake in the morning, he'd already be up and gone.

On the few nights that he didn't go back to work after

dinner, he was so tired that he'd fall asleep in the big leather recliner.

We didn't make love once during those two weeks. And I just couldn't find the right time to ask him about his mother and all the baby graves. Or bring up Cathy. Or the wheelchair. Or finding a job.

Then came the news: he was moving cattle. Again.

I'd be alone. Again.

"Jack, I want to send out some résumés to the local schools about teaching this fall. Can you make a list for me?"

He didn't say anything to my request.

"And do I have to eat dinner in the big house?" I asked.

"Well, I would think JT would expect it, Beth. Why? Don't you want to eat over there?"

This was hard for me to tell him; after all, it was *his* father. "It's just that he asked me if I was pregnant yet the last time you were gone," I told him, blushing.

"I'll talk to Glenn," Jack replied curtly.

I wasn't sure what Glenn had to do with anything. But I could tell by the way Jack said it that the discussion was closed.

~~~~~~

One hot summer weekend in early August, Jack suggested an "overnight," out in the country. He told me about a place near the river where we could camp.

"The river will almost always give up a fish or two, and if not, we can eat beans," bragged *my* cowboy. "And we can skinny dip the dust off of us, among other things," he said with a wink.

Jack planned everything: the gear, the food, and even the beer.

"Mmmm, warm beer," I snickered, watching him shove a

six-pack in the saddlebag.

"You'll see," he replied, a smile playing around his lips.

We left just after midday on Friday. It took us several hours on horseback to get to this legendary spot of his. The ride was hot. Buttercup and his horse, Guy, had to be walked every hour or so. Sometimes Jack would ride alongside me, but other times he rode ahead. He certainly was a handsome figure in the saddle. With his back straight, his cowboy hat, and a denim shirt with the sleeves rolled up, he reminded me of the Marlboro Man in the cigarette commercials. His hair curled over his shirt collar, and when he looked at me with those Big-Sky-blue eyes, he could still trip my heartbeat.

It was late, but there was still some daylight when we finally arrived at the campsite. Jack was right—it was beautiful. The fading sunset cast a golden glow on the water. The mountains looked close enough to reach, if only we rode a little while longer. There was a stand of trees with enough fallen branches for firewood. The "sleeping area" was a flat spot protected on one side by one of those numerous rock outcroppings. It was obvious he had been here before from the blackened firepit rimmed with small stones.

After unpacking the gear, unsaddling the horses, and hobbling them so they could graze but not run off, Jack explained how he planned to chill the beers.

"Beth, grab that mesh bag over there," he directed, pointing to a woven pouch on top of the sleeping bags. "And now the beer," he instructed.

Putting the cans in the bag, he walked along the river's edge, looking for something.

"Is there an ice box over there?" I teased him.

"Nope, something handier," he said. "Here we go."

Jack dropped the beer-loaded bag into a deep moving pool of the river. Then, with a strand of thin rope, he tied the bag to a low branch overhanging the water.

"Very clever," I praised him.

Next, he rigged up a fishing line to lure one of those famous fish to our frying pan. It was obvious that he'd done all of this a time or two.

As I watched him, I wondered if he had been out here with Glenn or one of the other men. *Or with another woman. Cathy?*

Shoving those thoughts aside, I searched through his bag of gear. "So, where's the tent?" I asked.

"Beth, darlin', we're sleeping under the stars," he announced. When he saw the look on my face, he quickly added, "Don't worry, we have sleeping bags and we'll be near the fire. That's all we need."

I had never done *anything* like this. My Girl Scout experience was limited to camping in cabins in a city forest preserve. If someone had told me a year ago that I would be camping out under the stars in Montana with a *real* cowboy, I would have asked them what they'd been smoking.

True to his word, he did catch a fish. I applauded my cowboy fisherman, but he only winked at me and then put me to work cutting up onions and potatoes while he cleaned the fish and started the fire. The firewood crackled and popped as it was consumed by the flames. Soon, the tantalizing aroma of fried fish with potatoes and onions set my mouth watering and my stomach growling. The beer wasn't ice-cold, but it was cold enough. And dinner was delicious. Something about the fresh air and the campfire smoke made it taste better than any stove or grill ever could.

After cleaning up from dinner, Jack watered and fed the horses. He secured them for the night and came back to camp. We zipped the sleeping bags together, kicked off our boots, and stretched out on top. It was still too warm to be covered up. Sparks occasionally showered the area around the firepit as the larger pieces of firewood collapsed inward. The cool mountain air felt so refreshing after the heat of the day.

Jack pulled me to him, kissing me and pulling my top off at the same time. Still nervous about having my clothes off in the great outdoors, I tried to push his hands away.

"What if someone comes by?" I whispered.

"There's *no one* around, Beth," Jack assured me. "Everyone from the ranch knew we were coming out here, and nobody would dare interrupt us. Glenn would make sure."

"Well, what about critters?" I asked timidly.

"Darlin', the *critters* are more scared of *you*. They won't come anywhere near the fire. And besides, the horses will warn us."

I listened. Over the softly crackling fire, I could hear the chomping of the horses grazing and their occasional stomping and snuffling. And, if I strained my ears, I could make out the gurgle of the river. It was *so* still. Billions of stars shimmered in the clear night sky. This beautifully different view of Big Sky Country left me breathless.

Jack was persistent, and soon his kisses and stroking made me forget everything else. Unlike that other time at Mount Rushmore, he was more insistent, confident he was going to have his way. Soon my jeans were off, the cool night air blowing gently over my bare legs. I briefly wondered what that would feel like on my bare behind.

I never found out, because soon Jack was partially on top of me, keeping me warm while another hard part of his body was making me hot. I completely forgot about being outdoors, never thought again about any critters, and only wondered once what the horses thought of our lovemaking. *Do horses think?*

I had to admit, only to myself, that there was quite a freedom in being naked outdoors.

~~~~~~

The next morning, Jack served a breakfast of coffee and campfire biscuits. The man was amazing. Eventually, we saddled the horses and headed toward the mountains. He told me he wanted to show me something very special, but he wouldn't say more.

It was a long ride on Buttercup, but when we finally reached some real, honest-to-goodness foothills of those enticing, inviting, mesmerizing mountains, it was so worth it. Jack tethered the horses, and we continued on foot. When I followed him around a big outcropping of large boulders, I saw his special surprise: old Indian carvings on a large flat-faced rock. The artwork was hidden away in a recess. Studying the worn carvings, we could decipher several horses and what looked like a bear. One scene might have been a buffalo hunt. Jack told me that Glenn had shown this to him as a young boy. It was a fairly secret place and I was honored to be shown this secluded treasure.

After the long ride back to our campsite, we were hot and dusty. It was one thing to be naked on the sleeping bag, in the dark, lost in passion. But to be naked…outdoors…in the daylight? And yet the water looked so inviting, I could certainly use a dunking, and Jack was right: there was no one around for miles.

~~~~~~

Jack eyed Beth swimming *au naturel*. Occasionally, he'd catch a glimpse of her breasts or her cute ass as she played in the water. Watching her gave him a hard-on.

~~~~~~

When I boldly climbed out of the water, Jack gave me a towel and a lusty look.

~~~~~~

Jack finally nailed Beth in the great outdoors. Not just once, but *twice*. She was so shy; Jack just loved bringing out her uninhibited side. Never had that problem with Cathy. Hell, she'd have been running around the campsite naked five minutes after they got here. He always worried whether he'd be able to get her clothes back *on her* when it was time to leave.

Although he told Beth that no one was around, he continually searched the range for any other riders while they were out today. Cathy had an eerie intuition, or more likely ranch-hand spies, to always know where he was.

But Beth enjoyed the water, as Jack figured she would since she loved to swim, once he assured her there were no snakes or fish. Of course there were, but she would never have gone in the water if he had told her the truth.

~~~~~~

The wonderful weekend, just the two of us, reminding me why I fell in love with this cowboy, *almost* made up for the news that he was, yet again, moving the cattle. At least this time, Glenn was staying at the ranch so I wouldn't have to dine alone with JT.

Another surprise happened while Jack was gone this time. Cathy came by the ranch. I wondered if she knew Jack was gone, but she said, "I've come a-callin' to see *you*."

Glenn made that funny sign, warding off the evil spirits, or whatever it meant, when she dismounted and loosely looped the reins around the nearest fence.

"I sure am sorry I haven't come by sooner, Elizabeth," she cooed, but made no excuses.

I started to invite her inside the little house for a cool

drink when Glenn blocked us and said we should go on up to the big house.

"Oh, *Hunky* Bear, we don't want to bother old JT now with our *girl talk*," Cathy said, practically batting her eyelashes at Glenn.

What? *Was she flirting with him?* It had no effect, though—Glenn ignored her, and behind her back, he frowned and shook his head.

We stood around the yard, with Glenn hovering, making the smallest of small talk. Cathy asked me again how Jack and I met. She mumbled something about staying in the clan. I had no idea what she was talking about. I wasn't sure I wanted to ask. When we had exhausted the chit-chat about how I was adjusting to Montana, the ranch, and riding, and the pauses bordered on uncomfortable, she turned to Glenn and said, "I guess I need to find my horse and giddy up."

As she rode out, I was still undecided as to whether I liked her or hated her. *How long ago was she Jack's leftovers?* And since my husband wasn't giving me any information, maybe I needed to corner Glenn for some answers.

~~~~~~

I went over to the big house to browse JT's library. I had exhausted my reading supply and hoped to find something of interest in his extensive collection. He'd offered many times, so I thought I'd finally take him up on it.

As I was leaving the library with a couple of books, I heard JT say, "No, not yet." When there was no further conversation, I realized he was on the phone. Then I heard him say, "Jackson says any time now." I stopped to eavesdrop since this involved Jack. And then JT said, "Yes, it sure will be nice to have the patter of little feet."

Oh, good grief. Not the "When will there be a baby?" talk

again. I scurried into the hallway and out the front door. What was I? Breeding stock?

I wanted to shout at JT, "It's difficult to get pregnant when my husband spends more time moving cows than he does with me!"

~~~~~~

Riding alone out on the range, Jack let his mind wander as the herd plodded toward their next pasture. He noted the lush grass growth, the light wind, and the sun low in the sky. *A good life*, Jack thought. A good life indeed.

Finding the dead cow sent a shock through him. It had obviously been dead for some time, and the coyotes and vultures had been working on it. Jack didn't hear a crying calf in the vicinity, so he figured the cow had not been bred. But not all the damage had been caused by the scavengers. Her belly had been split from under her forelegs to her rump. He hated to think it, but the cut looked almost surgical. Bears or cougars ripped with multiple slashes. Wolves attacked in a pack with many bites and tears. No wild animal that he knew of made one long, neat-edged slice. This was a deliberate mutilation.

Jack knew he'd have to talk to some of the other ranchers and see if they were having any problems. Jack shook his head, sickened by the disturbing sight. Anxiety rose in his gut as he thought about telling JT what he had found.

~~~~~~

I could tell that Jack was tired when he came home this time. *And weren't the cows tired too?*

"Why do you move the cows around so much? Doesn't that wear them out?" I asked.

"We're not moving the same cattle, Beth," he told me with a new edge to his voice.

~~~~~~

In the last weeks of August, we had reestablished the routine of our early days. More sex. Some riding in the afternoons. But now Jack brought a rifle along on our rides. When I asked him why, he just shrugged and said, "We're getting into bear season. They come down from the mountains and start eating everything in sight, to put on fat for the winter. And some will still have their cubs with 'em. Dangerous mamas."

The blemish on our bliss was that Cathy rode in more frequently. I even saw Jack arguing with her one day, and it looked like he gave her a little shove. *What was that about?*

And the other bit of news was about the wedding reception he had promised. Labor Day weekend. As a surprise to me, he had already contacted Lucy and made travel arrangements for her to fly to Bozeman. When did he have time to do that? I couldn't wait to get Lucy on the phone and find out how she managed to keep *that* secret.

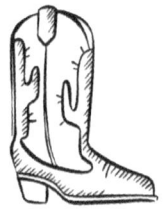

CHAPTER 18

The Big Weekend was just a few days away. My long-awaited, long-promised wedding reception, which I found out would just be a *very small* part of the annual Labor Day Weekend Rodeo on the Juddson Ranch. *Did it matter? I don't know anyone here. At least Lucy will be here.*

I wanted to help or at least be a part of the planning. But this weekend had been an event for many years, so the house staff knew what to do and who to call to make it all happen.

Sarah didn't need any help, and I realized I was just in the way when I went to ask her. The outdoor work of setting up the corrals for the rodeo events required a knowledge and strength I didn't possess. I was reminded, once again, that I was an outsider. All the planning went on around me...but without me.

~~~~~

Jack and I made a fast trip into Bozeman to pick up Lucy at the airport. It was so good to see her. She was in awe as we started driving through those many gates when I told her this was all Jack's ranch.

"You got yourself a *real* cowboy, Liz."

I just blushed. Little did she know.

~~~~~~

JT had suggested that Lucy stay in one of the six bedrooms in the big house, but I insisted that she stay in our little house. Although I knew Lucy could hold her own with JT, I wanted her close to me these few days. Mattress, bedding, nightstands, and a dresser were moved over to furnish one of our spare bedrooms.

Jack dropped us off, saying he had work to do. I gave Lucy a quick tour and showed her the spare room. Back downstairs, we grabbed a couple of beers and settled in the living room to catch up.

"Are you happy, Liz?" Lucy started.

"Most of the time, yes," I told her honestly. When one of her beautiful dark eyebrows went up, I hurried to explain, "Jack's gone a lot, moving cattle. He can be gone for days. But a few weeks ago, we went camping and it was great. Just the two of us." I blushed.

"Sex in the great outdoors, huh? Look at you, Liz." Lucy giggled. "What else have you been doing?"

"Well, there's a small town—get this—named Juddson. Can you believe it? I married Little Joe Cartwright."

"No, Liz, I think he's a younger version of Adam, with those dark looks. Definitely not Hoss." Lucy laughed.

It was *so* good to have her here. Someone to talk to. About *everything*.

"There's an ex-girlfriend who hangs about," I confided. "*Cathy* is a sexy blonde and I'm sure you'll see her this weekend," I remarked sourly.

"Is Jack unfaithful, Liz?"

"No, I don't think so. No. It's just that she was in his past. And I'm not sure how long ago that was. Oh, and Jack's dad, JT, is in a wheelchair."

"What? How'd that happen?"

"I still haven't found out. When I asked Jack, all he would say was that it was an accident. And Jack's mother died in childbirth when she was thirty-four. There's a small graveyard here on the property," I shared.

We sipped our beers in silence until Lucy asked, "Did you find a teaching job?"

"No. I couldn't even find a list of schools to send my résumé to. The nearest town, the one named after them, is the quintessential 'one-horse town.' It *had* an elementary school, but it's closed now. You saw how far away Bozeman is. Besides, I don't think Jack or JT want me to teach."

"Why, what did they say? What do they expect you to *do*? Cook and clean for a bunch of ranch hands?"

"Jack doesn't say anything one way or the other. But every time I ask him for a list of schools, he either ignores me or he goes off to move some more cows. One time when I had dinner alone with JT, Jack was out moving cows, JT said that I didn't need to work. I told him I may not *need* a job, but I *want* a job. Get this—JT said, 'When you have some young'uns, you can teach them how to read.'"

"He said that?" Lucy asked, astounded. "What a dick!"

"Lucy, I thought I'd at least cook and keep house for Jack. He eats almost every meal at the big house. And there are servants who do all the cooking, cleaning, and laundry. I have absolutely nothing to do. I'm not allowed to go riding by myself. I tried that once."

"What happened?"

"I fell off my horse, which bolted back to the ranch. Jack came looking for me and was very angry that I *disobeyed* him." Seeing the look in her eye, I quickly added, "But we've gotten past that. It's just not what I had expected. But enough about me. Tell me all about Arizona."

And with that, Lucy entertained me with stories of moving into her apartment, exploring the campus, and checking out the college bars. *Sounded like a lot of fun.*

~~~~~~

The weekend was one long party. They roasted a steer. A whole steer! Troughs full of beer on ice were everywhere. Harder liquor was discreetly passed around in flasks and bottles. The men did crazy things with their horses: chasing poor little calves and tying them up; wrestling steers; riding bucking broncos. There were bareback challenges and barrel races. Even the women competed. Fun to watch, but I would *never* be in that league of riding.

Friends and neighbors along with their ranch hands came, mostly on horseback, some in jeeps. It was hard for me to keep track of Jack, but he *was* the host, and I did have Lucy to keep me company.

~~~~~~

Cathy cornered Jack as he was coming out of the large barn. She cozied up to him and, slurring slightly, told him she had a wedding present for him.

"I'll just bet you do, honey," Jack told her. He well remembered what she could do with those full, pouty lips. Luckily, one of the ranch hands was hurrying toward him, so he turned to Cathy and said, "Now don't drink too much, and try to behave yourself." He didn't wait for a reply.

Later, Jack saw her draped all over one of the hands from another ranch. He appeared to be holding her up with a good grip around her narrow waist. *Good, let her be his problem.*

Jack spent some time talking to the other ranchers about the cattle mutilation. No one else had experienced anything like that. He was beginning to believe it was a cougar or bear. Except for that split belly.

~~~~~~

I had to leave Lucy on her own when I was summoned by JT to meet some of the neighbors. Jack being nowhere in sight, I gritted my teeth and made my way over to where he was "holding court" in his chair on the wide porch. *He best not make any "baby remarks" to these neighbors*, I thought, and then asked myself, *and if he does, what would I do?*

But JT was behaving himself today and one could *almost* like him when he turned on that Juddson charm.

~~~~~~

Lucy wandered off to watch the rodeo and check out the cowboys. Some fine prime beef was being shown off today. As she was about to move down to another corral to watch the women's barrel race, she overheard an obviously over-inebriated woman mention Jack. Getting closer, she could see that the sloppy drunk was blonde and sexy. Cathy? Lucy deliberately eavesdropped on the two women. Cathy mumbled "bloodlines" and a few minutes later muttered "crawling back."

Whatever was this drunken bitch talking about? Lucy thought.

Finally, the more sober of the two said to the blonde, "Cathy, you better ease up on the booze. Your tongue is way too loose, girl."

Lucy waited around to see if the blonde bimbo would spew anything else, but a couple of hands came up to them and the conversation shifted back to the rodeo events.

~~~~~~

Later that evening, Lucy and I escaped to my house, leaving the die-hard drinkers to stagger around. I made sure Jack knew where we were going. Settling in the living room with some cold drinks, Lucy launched right in.

"Liz, I saw Cathy today."

"Not surprising. Everyone for miles was here. JT introduced me to so many people, I'll never remember them all. And maybe I'll not see any of them again 'til next year." I giggled.

"Liz, I overheard Cathy talking to another woman about you and Jack."

"Me? What'd she say about me?" *The bitch*, I thought.

"She said that the Juddsons *always* have to marry one of their own. Something about keeping the bloodline intact. What the heck does that mean?" Lucy asked.

"That's creepy," I said with a shiver. "I have no idea what she's talking about. Was she drunk?"

"Oh yeah. Big time. Her friend warned her to watch her liquor and her mouth," Liz relayed.

"Was that it? Did she say anything else?" *Did I really want to know?*

"Get this," Lucy started. "That blonde bitch said Jack will never give her up for good. And that once Jack gets you pregnant, he'll have made JT happy and then Jack will come crawling back to her."

We were both quiet for a while. *Very sure now I hate Cathy.*

"Just drunk talk, Liz," Lucy assured me. "Jack loves you. He'd be a fool to mess around with her. She's trouble with a capital T."

~~~~~~

I was sure glad when the weekend was over. It was so great to see Lucy and I would miss her all over again. It was fun staying up and talking until two a.m. But there were too many people at the rodeo that I didn't know. I hardly saw Jack. Saw too much of Cathy. After what Lucy told me, Cathy was everywhere I looked. I'm just so out of place here. Still just a *city* girl. I might have the outfits, but I would never be a cowgirl. *And really, did I want to be?* I missed the city with all its museums and galleries. And I sure missed swimming, where I could pound the water and work out all my problems.

~~~~~~

About a week later, when I went to brush Buttercup, I ran into Glenn.

"Did you enjoy the rodeo, Elizabeth?" he asked.

"It was something. Quite a shindig," I replied noncommittally.

When it didn't look like he was just passing through, I thought maybe it might be a good time to get some answers.

"Can I ask you something, Glenn?" Without waiting for a reply, I blurted, "How did JT end up in the wheelchair? Jack said he had some kind of accident about ten years ago but won't say anything else."

After a long enough pause that I thought he wouldn't respond, Glenn finally told me, "Jack *caused* the accident that injured JT and put him in that chair. Jack carries a ton of guilt around over it, and JT will never let him forget it."

I didn't say anything, hoping my silence would encourage Glenn to tell me more.

"You see, Jack has always wanted to change things. Innovate. Make ranching easier. More profitable. He was loading hay bales in one of the outbuildings. Decided to try out a shortcut. Instead of stacking the bales one high, he stacked them two deep on the conveyor. At first, when he turned on the belt, it looked like it would work. I was up in the loft, unloading as fast as I could while Jack double-stacked. We really didn't know JT was anywhere in the area until he came into the barn shouting at Jack, 'What the fuck are you doing?' and strode over to switch off the conveyor. Bad luck would have it, at that very minute the bales started slipping, and they all fell on top of JT. Crushed his vertebra and pelvis. Caused some irreversible nerve damage. And JT's been in that chair ever since."

I was horrified by the story, and at the same time my heart went out to Jack. It was an accident. JT was in the wrong place at the wrong time. It might have just as easily been Jack.

When I asked Glenn how Jack managed to avoid the tumbling bales, he said, "It was just one of them *freak accidents*. Hard to explain exactly how it happened or even why it happened. It just happened."

After this revelation, I didn't want to ask about Cathy. Or about Ida Mae and all the baby graves. The story I'd just heard was not what I'd expected, but it sure did clear up a lot. Explained why JT didn't trust Jack around the ranch. And why he wouldn't let Jack implement any new procedures or techniques.

"Tread lightly, Elizabeth," Glenn was saying. "This is a very touchy subject on the Juddson ranch. Don't pick at it or try to solve it."

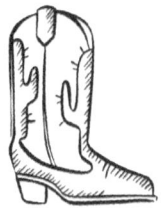

CHAPTER 19

One night in the middle of September, I woke up, and Jack was not in bed. Getting up, I couldn't find him anywhere in the house. The green-eyed monster planted images of him off in a dark corner with Cathy. I pulled on jeans, tucked in my sleep tee, and went downstairs to pull on my boots.

There was a light coming from one of the barns, and I headed in that direction. Though I had to know, I dreaded what I might find. Did he think he could marry me and keep Cathy "on the side"? *Maybe she wasn't so much a leftover as she was dessert.*

As I got closer to the barn, I heard a strange noise. An animal noise. I crept through the barn door, and there was Jack lying on the straw next to a mare. Then I saw the horse convulse and realized she was having a contraction. *She's about to give birth!* This was the late foal that Jack and Glenn had talked about at dinner.

Noticing me inching my way in, Jack asked me, "Well, now that you're here, would you give me a hand?"

I nodded but wondered if I could really be any help.

"Hold her head, and try and keep her calm. I'm going to

have to help her. The foal is breeching."

The shock must have shown in my eyes, but as the horse went into another contraction, I scurried around her, close to her head, and did as Jack instructed.

He went to her back end, took off his shirt, and proceeded to stick his arm...well, oh my goodness. She didn't seem to mind. Maybe she knew on some level he was trying to help.

The next thing I saw was a pair of skinny legs being pulled out by my cowboy midwife husband.

Well, I didn't care if it was kittens, puppies, foals, or human babies—the miracle of birth was amazing to witness.

The rest of the tiny horse came along: two more legs, a body, and a head. Mama mare was doing wonderfully. I kept praising her, telling her she had a beautiful baby.

When it was over, afterbirth expelled, mama back on her feet and baby trying to stand on wobbly legs, I looked at Jack and wondered if this entire ranch was just all about babies.

~~~~~~

In keeping with me *not* having any babies just yet, a few days later I told Jack I wanted to go into town. I needed more birth control pills as there were only enough to get me through October.

By the time Jack took me to see the family doctor in Juddson, it was the beginning of October and I desperately needed a refill. The way Jack had described the family doctor, Doc Hardin, all I could think of was Marcus Welby, MD. I wasn't too far off. He was older than Glenn, but younger than JT. His white hair made guessing his age difficult, but his eyes were clear and sparkled with life. He slapped Jack on the back and, with a surprisingly firm grip, shook my hand.

"Come in, come in," he said as he ushered us into his crowded office. Papers and files, books, and pictures cluttered the room. "Well, Jack, she sure is a pretty young thing," he said, as if I wasn't sitting right there. "Still honeymooning?" he asked with a grin.

Jack just smiled and gave what appeared to be an affirmative nod. I blushed.

"How's JT? Ornery as ever, I suppose," he babbled. "What can I do for you two today?"

I pulled my last birth control pack from my purse and slid it across his desk. "I need a refill. For six months please."

"Jack, you approve of this?" Doc Hardin asked. "You're planning on giving JT grandkids, aren't you?"

Jack again just sort of nodded. All of a sudden, the usually "take-charge" cowboy I'd married was being kowtowed by the family doctor.

"Of course, just not yet," I told him.

"Well, Elizabeth, I will need to do an examination. And we'll have to order a pregnancy test. Jack, come back in about a half-hour," Doc Hardin ordered.

Back at college, the University Health Center practically *gave* birth control pills away. I had figured the doctor wouldn't renew the prescription without an exam, but I dreaded it anyway. Of course, it would have been worse if he had let Jack stay; I couldn't imagine being on the exam table, legs wide apart, feet in the stirrups, with Jack in the room.

Once again dressed, while waiting in Doc Hardin's office for the magic slip of paper that would allow me to have worry-free sex for at least half a year, I studied the medical degrees and certificates tacked to the walls. There were also many pictures of newborn babies. I guessed he had delivered them all.

The door opened with a rush, and the doctor came around to sit at the desk.

Before he could start, I blurted out, "I'm not pregnant, so there's no need for a pregnancy test."

"When was your last period, dear?" Doc Hardin asked.

I stopped to think. *When was it?* It was before the rodeo weekend. Counting back, that was five—no, almost six weeks ago.

"A little over a month," I lied.

"Best to do the test, Elizabeth," he said, handing me the plastic cup. "There's a bathroom down the hall."

"How long will it take to get the results?"

"Ten days to two weeks. Have to send it off to Bozeman," he informed me as Jack walked into the office.

I tried to not think about possibly being pregnant. I was not ready. I wanted to have Jack's children, but not yet. Once there was a child, I would be forever tied to the ranch. Too bad Ida Mae lost all those babies. Another brother or two for Jack and the pressure would have been off me to provide the heir.

I'd been late before, I calmed myself. Before Jack. When I hadn't had sex. One time in college, I skipped an entire month. I was stressed with classes, not eating much, and swimming twice a day. But not pregnant.

It was the same thing now, I was sure. Stressed over this new life on the ranch: JT, all the secrets, and weeks of horseback riding. I just couldn't be pregnant.

~~~~~~

Through an open window one warm day in the second week of October, I watched a car motor into the homestead. To my complete surprise, Doc Hardin stepped out of the fancy car. *I was expecting a phone call, not a house call. This was a private matter, right?*

Old JT must have seen him drive up too, because before I could put down the book I was reading, JT had rolled himself out onto the porch.

"Jim, what brings you out?" JT hollered.

"Checking up on you, you ornery old bastard," Doc Hardin yelled back.

"Well, as you can see, I'm fit as a fiddle. But since you made the trip out, come in, come in," JT invited.

"Is Jack around?" I heard Doc Hardin ask.

Jack must have been close enough to have seen or heard the car. Walking toward the porch, he replied, "I'm right here, Doc. Something wrong?"

"No, no. Good news. Grab Elizabeth and meet us inside," Doc Hardin declared.

I headed out the door as Jack walked toward our house. Together, we hurried to the big house, entering just as JT was offering Doc Hardin a whiskey.

"There she is," Doc Hardin says. "Well, we're all here. Congratulations, Jack, you're gonna be a daddy."

What? No!

JT gave a loud hoot. "Damn! Great news, Jim, great news."

Jack turned to me and saw my face. Whether to hide it from JT or to comfort me, I wasn't sure, but he gathered me up in his arms and whispered, "I love you, Beth."

Congratulations were shouted. To Jack. To JT. Glenn came in to find out why the doctor was making a visit, and he got in on the back-slapping and hand-shaking. Jack kept a protective arm around me, possibly worried I'd run off in hysteria.

I had told him about the pregnancy test and insisted I wasn't pregnant, but didn't confide that I was running a little late with my period. And I had reminded him, again, that I wanted to wait a year or two before having a baby.

So much for that plan. It had to be the weekend we went camping. I had forgotten to bring the pills and, although I took them as soon as we got back, apparently that wasn't enough protection.

"I want you to come to the office next week and we'll figure out how far along you are, Elizabeth," Doc Hardin instructed.

"Okay, Doc, sure," Jack answered for me.

~~~~~

JT was in seventh heaven. He would tell anyone who would listen that I was pregnant. If there wasn't anything for me to do before, it was worse now. I was forbidden to ride Buttercup. They coddled me every chance they could. It was stifling.

JT had the family cradle brought down from the attic and delivered to the little house. It was a beautiful handmade wooden piece with detailed carvings on either end. JT told me more than once that Jack had slept in that crib after he was born.

I was instructed to start thinking of colors for the nursery. They would move me temporarily into the big house while one of the ranch hands painted. Jack needed to take me into Bozeman to shop for maternity clothes.

~~~~~

Three days later, I woke up in the night with a sticky feeling between my legs. My period had started. I wasn't pregnant, as I had tried to tell Jack and Doc Hardin. I never had been.

I tried not to be too happy while everyone else was destroyed by the news.

The evening that Doc Hardin made his house call, I told Jack, "I've been late before. It could be all the horseback riding. And you know I've lost weight over the summer. You just commented on how bony I am the other night."

He had grinned at the recent memory.

I didn't want to tell Jack I was troubled. But I was. He was gone so much. And I didn't enjoy dinners alone with JT. I wanted to teach. There was nothing for me to do. I missed going to the city; missed the museums and the Art Institute. I missed swimming and I desperately missed Lucy.

~~~~~~

A week later, and after another exam just to make sure I hadn't been pregnant, Jack and I sat in Doc Hardin's office. I insisted on the prescription for the pills.

"Doc, how could you have told us Beth was pregnant?" Jack demanded.

"Jack, these tests are not 100% accurate. Could have been a trace amount of the hormone they're testing for, and some tech thought it was enough to call it," Hardin tried to explain.

"Well, old JT is ready to sue somebody," Jack warned.

Hardin thought on that for a few moments, then deftly changed the subject. "Well, Elizabeth, you are plenty healthy for children. But I don't want to see you on the pill for any length of time. I'll renew for six months," he reluctantly agreed. "A young filly like you should be having babies every year," he added.

If I had been standing near him, I think he would have slapped me on the rump to emphasize his comment.

~~~~~~

On the ride back to the ranch, I briefly wondered about my tipped uterus. Even after two exams, Doc Hardin never mentioned it. *Could it have somehow righted itself?* I made a mental note to see about a doctor in Bozeman. *Maybe even a woman doctor.*

CHAPTER 20

In late October, the men—all but JT, that is—went on the Annual Elk Hunt. Jack said he'd be gone almost a week. I was beginning to realize that ranch life was lonely for women. Most of the ranchers' wives cooked, cleaned, ran the household. I wasn't allowed to do any of *that*.

Early on, I had asked if there wasn't some work on the ranch I could do. Whatever they were thinking, they didn't utter it out loud. But the looks on Jack and Glenn's faces said it all. This was "man's work," and I'd just be in the way. I asked about paperwork or bookwork. No; they had an accountant from Bozeman who came out once a month to go over JT's bookkeeping.

The time by myself was long and lonely. I could interrupt one of the hands to accompany me on a ride, but that was uncomfortable for both of us.

I visited the library in the big house often. It was while everyone was away that I stumbled on the family Bible. It was one of those big old-fashioned Bibles with colored pictures of various Old Testament stories: Lot's wife being turned into a pillar of salt; Moses bringing down the tablets and finding the false idol. This Bible had a "family history" page in the very front. Written in a fancy script that was difficult to read, there were at least four generations of Juddsons listed, along with who they married and the names of their children.

There, in the middle of the previous generation, I saw my last name: Mitchell. First name: Mary. *What? I'm related to the Juddsons somehow?* A chill went down my spine when I thought about the mystery around my father. About my mother's hesitation to tell me about him. *If only she were still alive and I could ask her.* Hearing a noise in the hallway, I quickly shoved the large book back into its spot on the shelf and left the room.

I begged off dinner in the big house that night. Let JT think I had *evening* sickness. Cathy's remarks about "staying in the clan" kept running through my mind. *Oh, dear God, what have I married into?* All the baby suggestions and hints were bad enough. Made me feel like the prize "brood mare" on the ranch. But now... *I might actually be related to Jack?* It was too much.

I slept fitfully with dreams of golden bulls chasing me in a field. I woke up late, lethargic and moody. Jack wouldn't be back for several more days, and Glenn had gone on the elk hunt as well. JT was the only one around, but I wasn't about to ask him. I wasn't sure I wanted to hear *his* explanation.

I moped around the house for the next couple of days, not caring if JT was expecting me for dinner. I vaguely remembered my mother telling me about her *cousin* Mary. I think she was my great-uncle's daughter. My mother's father, my grandfather, had a brother. But this Mary had died years ago. I needed to get a better look at that family tree page in the Bible to figure out if there was a relationship. *It was probably a coincidence, right?*

Jack got back the next day, earlier than I had expected him. Did he sense trouble on the home front and return early?

"We shot two large elk. That's plenty of meat for everyone," he told me, not sounding especially pleased, as he stored his rifles in the gun cabinet. Dropping his duffel bag filled with very dirty clothes, he turned to me. "I'm sorry, Beth, I need to move some hay."

Now they're moving hay! I wasn't sure how I felt toward Jack. Had he specifically been looking for me just to "marry one of his own," as Lucy had quoted Cathy? Cathy asking, "How did Jack find you?" made me think he did. After all, *he* found *me* in the bar on campus. Had he been watching or, worse yet, *stalking* me? It was too awful to think about. Had his uncle been watching me at the university? I got a chill just thinking about it.

~~~~~~

Jack sensed that Beth was not happy to see him. Something was off. As if he didn't have enough problems to deal with.

On the elk hunt, they had come across another mutilated cow. Same slicing pattern as before. No tracks. No sign of any wild animals in the area. No one could figure it out. Everyone was spooked. After Glenn shot the second elk, they all agreed to head back.

Confronting JT about what he did or *didn't* say to Beth wouldn't do any good and would just lead to another argument with him. Beth would surely not be any happier when he told her he had to move all the herds in, closer to the ranch, for winter.

Jack had been gone almost a week, and even though he was tired, he wanted Beth. She still was a bit off, almost distant, but he wanted to make love to her, and Jack could be very persuasive. It took some kissing and a lot of fondling, but eventually Beth relaxed and let him have his way. She must have missed him, too, because she was wet when he entered her.

Beth had told him in the past that he took her to a place she'd never been before. She timidly told him once that she nicknamed the intense feeling *pleasure point*. Sometimes he thought his heart would burst when he thought about how he loved this shy woman. Beth had taken Jack someplace he had never been before, too: totally 100% in love.

As much as Jack hated leaving their warm bed, there was a lot of work to be done before the snow came. *Never-ending*, he thought. That was life on a ranch. He wanted to get in one more hay cutting, but the nights were starting to get chilly. Any day now, there would be a frost, and then it would be too late. The herds needed to be moved closer to the hay storage lean-tos not only for protection from the harsh winter weather but also for protection from "the mutilator," as he'd come to call the cow killer. Thank goodness that last mare had finally foaled. That was one of the latest they'd had in quite a while.

His thoughts returned to Beth. Even though things were still a bit strained between them, he hoped that she would tell him what was bothering her. *Women!* Not ever likely to solve that mystery, he headed to the big house for breakfast and to talk to Glenn about which vehicles and what equipment needed repairs or maintenance immediately.

~~~~~~

As the nights got colder and the sky threatened snow, I dreaded the oncoming winter. Jack was busy; too busy to spend much time with me. I needed to take another look at that Bible and get a better idea of the Mitchell-Juddson connection. Not wanting to confront Jack until I had more information, but remembering the whirlwind romance, as Lucy called it, I couldn't help but wonder if, instead of love at first sight, it was more of a planned ambush. After all, Jack's uncle was in the background and maybe he had been watching me as well. *Good grief, are Jack and I somehow related?* It was all too creepy to contemplate.

I didn't want to burden Lucy with any of this. The last time I talked with her, she was flat-out busy with end-of-the-semester projects and papers. Besides, I didn't want to hear her say, *"Well, Liz, I kinda told you so. What did you know about Jack besides his rugged good looks and expertise in the bedroom?"*

And all this pressure about having a baby. What was I? Breeding stock? New blood to improve the genetic strain? Or old blood, which might explain all of Ida Mae's dead babies. Did *she* "marry in the clan"? I muddled along with all those questions bouncing around my mind like loose pinballs.

~~~~~~

All it did in November was snow. Not a lot each time, but every second or third day, an inch or so fell until there was a good half-foot of snow on the ground. I could appreciate the beauty of the snow on the surrounding land. With the mountains as a backdrop, when the sun was shining, it was breathtaking.

~~~~~~

The ranch hands had mounted snow blades on a couple of the jeeps and smaller scoop blades on an ATV or two, so paths were made between the big and little houses and to the surrounding barns and buildings. Still, Jack cursed the snow because it made it more difficult to get out to the herds. He cursed the cold because it made it more difficult to work on the machinery. And he cursed it all because it made it more difficult to go into Juddson or anywhere else.

~~~~~~

Thanksgiving was strained with just the four of us. There was plenty of food, but very little conversation—although JT would always bring up *something* about the ranch. Jack would then try and promote a new technique or idea, to which JT inevitably found some reason to explain why it would never work on this ranch. Glenn was stuck being the peacemaker, and I just mumbled monosyllabic responses when necessary. It wasn't a long holiday weekend, either. The very next day, Jack and Glenn went back to work.

~~~~~~

In early December, the weather moderated for a few wonderful days. Temperatures above freezing and plenty of sunshine melted the snow. Here and there, you could see patches of grassy brown earth. Jack took me riding one of those days. Said it might be a while before I could get back out on Buttercup, and it would be good for both of us. He was right about seeing the land from the back of a horse. This was a beautiful spot. It was difficult to have brooding, suspicious thoughts while enjoying the sunshine and fresh air. And, if for only a little while, it was nice to get away from the houses and have Jack all to myself.

It was also during this weather interlude, on the pretense of borrowing more books, that I was able to spend some time in the library. Finding the Bible again, I studied the family history page in detail. Deciphering the fancy cursive handwriting, my heart sank.

It was true: my aunt had married JT's brother!

CHAPTER 21

Short days. Long nights. They might have been very enjoyable if only Beth would tell Jack what was wrong. *Something* happened when he was on the elk hunt. Since Glenn had been with Jack, they could only speculate. Even JT had commented that Beth was unusually quiet. Asked pointedly if she was feeling all right.

Jack knew this life was not for everyone. They were certainly isolated on the ranch, way out here in the foothills. But they had everything they needed right here. He preferred to think of it as self-contained and self-sufficient rather than remote and miles from anywhere. But to Beth, it might feel too secluded, too far from a town. With winter starting, she might be feeling it even more. Jack wondered how he could squeeze in a long weekend in Bozeman to cheer her up. *If* that was even the problem.

As if things weren't complicated enough, Cathy rode over on her snowmobile several times. She had this ridiculous—if not warm—fake fur coat that made her look twice her size. How she even managed the snow sled while wearing that bulky thing was anyone's guess. But, knowing Cathy, instead of any kind of control over the machine, she probably just aimed it at her destination. *One of these winters, someone's gonna find her between here and there with her neck broken.* Jack just hoped she was steering clear of the cattle. *Crazy bitch.*

~~~~~~

It was a few weeks until Christmas, and the big house was getting decorated. Evergreen garlands draped the porch railings. Beth could just imagine what was happening on the inside.

Jack came home unexpectedly one morning. He hollered up the stairs, "Beth, come down and give me a hand, would you?"

Hurrying down, I found a real tree, stuck halfway in—or halfway out, depending on your view of the front door.

"A tree! Oh, Jack, thank you," I cried as I threw my arms around him.

He took the opportunity to hold me tight and steal a passionate kiss. Something we'd been doing little of recently.

It was a small tree, but it was a real tree. Untangling myself from Jack, I raced back up the stairs to the spare bedroom, which still stored some of my boxes. Finding the two I wanted, I quickly brought them down.

"Hey, I thought you were going to help me," Jack complained.

"I am, I am. Let's bring it in," I said excitedly.

Jack went out the back door and around the house to the front door. He got into a position to push while I started to pull, and, with a grunt and a whoosh, the tree was in.

"It's lovely, Jack," I praised him as he righted it and stood it in a prominent place in the living room.

"Here, wait. There's more," he teased. From those deep pockets of his Marlboro Man jacket, he pulled out a bag of popping corn and two bags of cranberries. *He hadn't forgotten.*

"The popcorn was easy. But I had to pilfer the cranberries from Sarah's pantry," he confessed with a grin.

"Can you stay and help me decorate it, Jack?" I asked hopefully.

"I can get you started, Beth," he laughed, shrugging off his coat.

Together, we opened the boxes I had brought down and, finding the lights in a tangle, we began our first Christmas together.

~~~~~~

On a trip to town, and with Glenn's help, I purchased a new pair of gloves for Jack. Since shopping—not to mention my available cash—was hard to come by, I did some baking. I conspired with Sarah to help, and she gave me the ingredients to make cookies. I even sweet-talked her into getting me some bananas. Using my mother's recipe, I baked several tiny loaves of banana nut bread to give as gifts.

~~~~~~

Beth knew that Jack had told JT, many times, to stop with the suggestions about having a baby. Did he listen? Did he ever listen to anything Jack said? Obviously not, because for Christmas, JT gave me what looked like two big walkie-talkie radios.

Upon opening the present and seeing the puzzled look on my face, JT boomed, "Jim Hardin says these are the latest and greatest: baby monitors." When he saw I was still not understanding, JT further explained, "One goes in the baby's room and the other in your room. Once you turn them on, you can hear if the young'un is crying or just cooing."

I was too polite to say anything, but I'm sure Jack saw the

clench of my jaw, knowing that I was not thrilled with the gift. *Why can't JT see this is the last thing we need right now?*

I was pleased, however, with the book Jack gave me: James Michener's *The Drifters*.

"It's been on the bestseller list," Jack informed me. "I thought this winter you could travel to Spain, Portugal, Morocco, and Mozambique," he suggested with a wink.

At first, I didn't understand, but, upon reading the flyleaf, I smiled at Jack. *He did listen.*

He made a fuss over the gloves, telling me how much he needed a new pair. And, of course, he loved the cookies and the banana bread.

~~~~~~

The days after Christmas were a good time for the newlyweds. Jack made love to Beth many times and she seemed happy. The ranch had settled into its winter torpor. Feeding and watering the cattle and the horses were about the only chores at this time of year. Too much snow for checking fences. Too cold to work barehanded on machinery. Almost too cold to coax vehicles to turn over.

But it was only a few days into the new year that Jack found out just how *unhappy* Beth truly was. He didn't know she could get *that* angry. It was something to see that kind of passion. Unfortunately, it was directed at him.

~~~~~~

Jack had come back to the little house for lunch, and he brought up the damned boots. Again.

"Beth, why aren't you wearing your boots?" he asked.

"They are muddy and I don't want to wear them in the house," I replied irritably.

"Use the boot scraper. Any loose mud, Ruby will sweep up," Jack told me.

That started it. The tension between us had been building up since the elk hunt. The baby monitors didn't help. Factor in the snow, the cold, and *that* time of the month, and everything that had been bothering me came out in a screaming fury.

"There's nothing for me do here. I can't cook for you. Or do your laundry. I'm not even allowed to clean our house. You're gone all the time. I'm alone. I have no friends. I'm too far away from anything. I miss shopping. I miss swimming." Without a pause, I blazed on. "And you can tell your father that I'll have a baby when I'm goddammed ready to have a baby," I screamed at Jack. But I didn't stop there.

"Are you fucking Cathy?" I demanded. Not waiting for a reply, I asked, "And what the fuck did she mean by 'How did he find you?' and 'staying in the clan'? Was our meeting *not* by chance but somehow planned? Was your uncle part of the plot?"

"Of course not," Jack shouted.

"Of course not *what*?" I shouted even louder.

"I am *not* fucking Cathy!"

Out of everything I had just said, *that* was the point he decided to defend.

"But you *had* fucked her in the past?" I accused him.

He looked at me as if trying to decide on the best reply.

I helped him make the decision. "I've heard her referred to as 'your leftovers' so I'm assuming you two were an item."

"It's all in the *past*," he fired back.

"Well, a stiff dick has no conscience in the *present*."

A very brief look of hurt flashed in those gorgeous eyes. "I would *not* do that to you, Beth," he quietly told me.

"And what about 'finding me'? We didn't meet by accident, did we?" I was still on the attack.

When Jack said nothing, it was the look on his face that confirmed my worst fears.

~~~~~~

Jack didn't want to lie to Beth, but, as angry as she was right now, telling her the truth wasn't a good idea either.

He was trying to figure out *what* to say. *How* to say it. He wanted to deny he *had* been looking for her, but he'd waited too long to reply.

~~~~~~

It was obvious Jack was trying to decide what to tell me. It didn't matter. It was too late. I was devastated. Stunned. Hurt. Disappointed. And mad at myself for being so damn gullible. Always believing the good in everyone.

"What other secrets have you kept from me?"

~~~~~~

Not answering Beth's question, Jack tried charm. "I was there to help my uncle and I met you. And I fell in love with you. And I still love you."

He hoped that would be enough, but her body language said it wasn't. Before turning her back on him and running for the stairs, he saw she was gut-punched. *Fuck.*

~~~~~~

I had been trying not to think the worst, but now I knew the worst was true. Jack had tracked me down. Sweet-talked me. Used that devilish charm. Seduced me. And what did I do? Fell head over heels for the cowboy and married him. *Why didn't I listen to Lucy?*

What should I do? What can I do? There was too much snow on the ground to leave. Besides, *how* would I leave? I didn't have my car. And even if I did, it would get stuck in the first mile. Buttercup could only take me so far. *And that would make me a horse thief, right?* They used to hang horse thieves in the old West. Maybe they still did. And then where would I go? I still had a little money, but was it enough to get away from here and start over somewhere?

I had no answers. I didn't have any idea what to do. But one thing was for sure: I couldn't do *anything* until winter was over.

Later, when I recalled accusing Jack of secrets, I realized I had been keeping a big one from him: I still hadn't told him about my tipped uterus.

~~~~~~

It was a cold winter. The ranch hands that stayed on all year said it was the coldest they could remember. And for me and Jack, it was not *just* the weather. Over the next several weeks, by some kind of unspoken agreement, we were not quite curt to each other, but we were not quite pleasant either. I thought of it as frosty politeness. I would go up to bed early to read. If I didn't fall asleep before Jack came up, I pretended to be asleep when he came to bed. Intimacy was not going to happen. And, as before, he was gone before I awoke. He didn't bother coming to the little house for lunch.

Over several snowy evenings in the middle of January, Jack cleaned the guns from the locked cabinet. He offered to show me how, but I was not interested. On most of these evenings, I would go upstairs, but once or twice I stayed downstairs, pretending to read while stealing glances at him as he worked. I could still get a flutter from his good looks and those bedroom-blue eyes. It was fascinating to watch his complete absorption in the task. Then I would think about how he came looking for me, and anger replaced the flutter.

~~~~~~

Jack knew Beth either faked sleep when he came to bed or, if he managed to catch her still awake, she turned her back on him. Mumbled she had a headache. *Right.* Woman's excuse since time immemorial. If he could just charm the panties off of her and remind her of the one honest thing they had, maybe they could get past all the accusations and mistrust.

Catching her stealing looks at him while he cleaned the rifles and shotguns gave him hope that she still had feelings for him. Warm ones. Not the icy daggers he had been receiving.

While he cleaned and oiled the guns, his mind still puzzled over the cattle mutilations. The killings had eased up; ranch hands hadn't found any more. He still thought it must be a bear. Since there'd been no new activity, it made sense.

CHAPTER 22

At the end of January, I told Jack I wanted my car. I didn't ask; I strongly suggested that his uncle drive it out in the spring. I felt a twinge from the hurt look on his face, but I didn't see another solution. He wouldn't, or *couldn't*, be honest with me about how we met. And until I knew the truth, I couldn't justify staying in Montana.

In early February, I was staring at my closet, looking at what I could take when I left Jack. Most of the clothes were "cowgirl" outfits that he had purchased. There were still a few things that I had brought with me to this godforsaken place. There was a large box in the corner that I had forgotten about, and I couldn't remember what was in it. Opening it, I saw a few personal items I hadn't been able to part with last May, but there was also the box my mother had left me.

With shaky hands, I took it out and opened it. Besides papers and some old photographs, there was a large, fat envelope addressed to me. I opened it and pulled out a half-dozen handwritten pages. Just seeing my mother's handwriting brought a tidal wave of nostalgia and homesickness crashing over me. Sitting on the floor, leaning against the bed, I began to read.

My Dearest Elizabeth,

If you are reading this letter, then I am gone. Do not grieve as I've had an interesting life. And having you for my daughter has been the best part!

For many years you asked about your father. I will finally tell you the story. I hope you won't judge me for the decisions I made. At the time, I believed that each one was either the <u>only</u> one open to me or the <u>best</u> one under the circumstances.

I'll start at the beginning. As you might remember, my father had one brother. They were very close. My uncle also had only one daughter. Her name was Betty.

Wait. What? My aunt's name was Betty, not Mary? My mother's name was Betty, right? I kept reading.

Your Aunt Betty and I were not only the same age, but also we looked a great deal alike. We could often fool our teachers, and others, as to which one of us was who. We had so much in common: both of us had lost our mothers at an early age and neither of us had siblings. We were more than cousins; Betty and I were like sisters. She was fun-loving and free-spirited, behaving almost scandalously. I'm not saying she was 'loose,' as was the term back then. No, it was more of a nature of doing wild stunts. She was an outrageous flirt. She was the first of any of us to wear a two-piece bathing suit and as soon as she could get her hands on one...a bikini! She got caught wading in Buckingham Fountain, but luckily escaped with only a warning. Another time, she would have been caught shoplifting from Marshall Fields, but sensed she was being observed and discreetly put the item back. She drank too much...well, you get the idea.

Besides working in Chicago and living in the Girls Friendly Society housing with Betty and two other friends, I also volunteered at the Chicago Serviceman's Club. The USO had been "decommissioned" after WWII and the CSC was started for the

Korean War soldiers. It was the start of the Korean War, the summer of 1950.

Many girls volunteered and it was against the rules to date any of the soldiers. They were very strict about that. We could socialize with them on the dance floor, but no dating off the dance floor. Ridiculously unrealistic, but very strict. Impossible to enforce, but they meant well. Trying to protect our virginities, I guess.

Being too young to help much during WWII, I was excited to do my part for these soldiers. Betty and I were 20 at that time.

Betty thought it would be a lark to switch names while we worked at the CSC. I was against the idea because I didn't fancy having the reputation that came along with her name. But she insisted it would be fun. Since the soldiers were always shipping in and shipping out, we could switch back any time.

"Please," she begged me, "it will be <u>so</u> much fun. We can even pretend we really are sisters."

It was hard to say no to Betty. <u>Because</u> she always was a lot of fun. So I became Betty Mitchell and she became Mary Mitchell.

Oh my, I thought. Did they not ever switch back? I read on.

At one Saturday night dance, Betty met a man who literally swept her off her feet. He would not take 'no' for an answer, asking numerous times for her phone number. He asked her out on a date at every Saturday night dance for weeks. And for weeks she turned him down. He even followed us home after the dances on at least two occasions and camped out outside our lodgings. It wasn't creepy, but very sweet. He was persistent, and eventually it paid off.

Betty finally broke the rules and went out with him. After a few weeks he told her he loved her and wanted to marry her. As soon as possible. Before he deployed.

Betty wanted to marry him. She was madly in love with him. But there were several problems. Her father, my uncle, would never allow it. She was only 20. A bigger problem in my mind was that this man knew her as Mary. Not Betty. I begged her to tell him the truth. I told her if he truly loved her, he would understand the joke and still love her as the real Betty. But she wasn't sure and she didn't want to risk losing him.

This man's name was James, and he was from a big cattle ranch in Montana.

The hair stood up on my neck as I recognized the similarity to my experience with Jack.

His older brother had received a deferment to stay and work on the ranch with their father. There was a third brother, a few years younger than James who planned to enlist. That brother had no desire to work the ranch in Montana.

Unbeknownst to me, Betty, as Mary, 'borrowed' my birth certificate, my social security card, and eloped with James. They were married a short three weeks before he was sent to Korea.

As cruel Fate would have it, about the time she learned she was pregnant, Betty also found out James had been killed in Korea. She was heartbroken.

I wanted desperately to switch our identities back, but I hated to pester her in her grief. Then the unthinkable happened. In an early November snowfall, she was struck by a drunk driver. Both she and the baby died instantly.

Then, the summer after Betty died, my father and my uncle were killed together in a horrible boating accident on Lake Michigan. I had never been so alone. So much loss.

I wanted to reclaim my name, except there was already a death certificate filed under Mary Mitchell, along with <u>my</u> social security number. Finding it all too confusing and difficult, I became Betty Mitchell forever.

But life went on. I continued working at the CSC. About a year after your Aunt Betty died, I met James' younger brother, Robert, at one of those Saturday night dances. It was mostly by chance. He asked a lot of questions about Mary and about me. He was particularly interested in Mary's pregnancy. I wasn't sure how Robert knew about that, unless Betty had written about it to James, and the family got the letter with his belongings. Robert asked me out, but there wasn't any 'spark' on my part, so we never dated. I never heard or saw him after he shipped out.

Then I met your father. Henry Freidel. Utterly charming. An officer and a gentleman. We fell in love at first sight. Such a silly saying, but it was true for us. He was older and was stationed at the Great Lakes Naval Station.

One night of heavy petting things went too far and well...I gave myself to him. We were careful after that first time and used 'protection' after that. But a month later, yep, I was pregnant. And not married. Of course, back then, being pregnant and unmarried was a terrible disgrace, especially for an officer. I wasn't the only girl in that predicament. Lots of girls were marrying servicemen on the hurry-up.

We thought we had time to plan a nice wedding. Having served during WWII and assisted with the demobilization that followed, he was able to spend this new war mostly stateside. He served his country this time by training sailors for their part in the war.

I thought there was time to solve the bigger problem of getting married as Betty instead of as Mary. I wanted my identity back. But how could I do that? How to tell your father?

But cruel Fate again had other plans. One morning, in a hurry on his way to work in a heavy rainstorm he lost control of the car on that treacherous 'outer drive' with those dangerous changeable lanes. He was killed instantly. We never got married, and sadly he never got to see what a beautiful baby you were. So when I always told you that he died before you were born, that part was true.

But never for one minute did I ever regret keeping you. Yes, there were times it was very difficult. Money was tight at first. But my father and my uncle had left me money. I was blessed in that.

So my love life was not much luckier than your Aunt Betty's. Your father was the love of my life, in spite of our short time together. I know that he really did love me, too.

I hope, my darling daughter, that you have much more luck in your love life than either I or your aunt did. Forgive me for not sharing the details of your birth with you sooner.

I regret that I will not be able to see you marry and have children of your own. But know that you will have...

All my love always
Mom

I'm a crying mess by the time I finish reading the letter. Selfish tears of sadness for myself; I so missed my mother. Selfless tears for my mother, for all the tragedy in her young life—losing her cousin, then her father and uncle. Losing my father. Not being able to live under her own name. I nursed a spark of anger toward my aunt for being so self-serving, stealing my mother's identity. Now I understood why my mother told me many times that your name is the most important thing you have.

But there were joyful tears as well. I was relieved that I was *not* related to these ranch people. There was only a gossamer connection of a long-dead aunt briefly married to Jack's long-dead uncle. No blood relation. No cousin that was a Juddson. *But do they* think *I am related?* If my mother had been successful in reclaiming her identity, the Juddsons would have believed that I was related. Did they know about the switch? Had my mother told Robert when she met him at CSC?

Why did the Juddsons need to find me? Jack came east specifically to find me, didn't he? Why did he have to be so damned charming? I had some answers, but I still planned to leave in the spring.

~~~~~~

Whenever there was a nice sunny day, I would put on my boots and hike to the barn to see Buttercup. Spending time brushing and grooming her was a task that brought me some contentment. Buttercup acted happy to see me, although her nuzzling might have been to get at the carrot or apple I would bring her. Putting my arms around her neck, giving her a hug, it would feel as if she was hugging me back when she dropped her long neck over my shoulder.

It would have been helpful to pour my heart out to Buttercup; tell her everything that was bothering me, talking out loud as if to a girlfriend. Just to have someone listen, not try to offer a solution. *Well, that's impossible—she's a horse.* I sure didn't see a solution to my mess. If I stayed on the ranch, married to Jack, would I ever trust him again? But if I left, where would I go? I had no home to go back to.

I couldn't unload on Buttercup for another reason: the barn wasn't always empty. I certainly wasn't about to share my problems with any of the ranch hands.

Jack knew where I was, spending time with Buttercup, but he didn't bother me. Glenn, on the other hand, offered no such courtesy.

On one occasion, Glenn offered more than polite pleasantries about the weather or the ranch. He asked me point-blank if I had stopped loving Jack.

The question startled me, and when I didn't answer right away, I hoped that Glenn would move on. But he waited patiently while I thought about what to say.

"Yes. I do still love him. But I'm not sure I can trust him,"

I told him honestly.

"And why is that?" he pried. When I didn't reply, he speculated, "Does it have to do with how you met Jack?"

"How much has Jack told you?" I asked.

"Enough," he confessed. "Let me tell you something about JT. And about Jack. I told you about JT's accident and how the two of them have been ever since. Some days, JT will run Jack ragged. Blames him for things that are beyond Jack's control. JT doesn't like it one bit, being stuck in that chair. Hates it. Blames Jack for that too. JT exerts control the only way he can: he takes advantage of Jack's guilt. JT can be a mean, spiteful old man, and I'm the only one who can tell him that to his face. After I do, he lightens up on Jack for a while, but it never lasts long."

I listened to Glenn, but most of what he said I had already figured out or personally observed.

"You see, JT never got over the death of his brother," Glenn continued. Seeing the surprised look on my face, he explained, "There was a third brother. A middle son, James, between JT and Robert. There was a new war, this time in Korea. JT believed it was his duty to go and was fixin' to get a deferment for James to stay on the ranch. The country still needed beef as much as it needed soldiers. But James *wanted* to go, and he applied for the deferment in JT's name. James happily went off to war but sadly never came back. JT never forgave himself for that."

I didn't say anything to this new information, but I thought I knew where the story was going.

Glenn continued, "What's all this got to do with you, you're wondering? Well, while James was in training, he met a girl and they got married, and *pregnant*, before he was shipped out. James was killed shortly after he got to Korea, and his wife and unborn child were killed in a car accident not long after. And this girl, James's wife, was *your* Aunt Mary."

Before I could react, Glenn hurried on, "Now, don't you be fretting, Elizabeth—this don't make you kin to the Juddsons. Nothing wrong with your aunt marrying Jack's uncle. Doesn't make you and Jack any kind of relatives."

I was not surprised by Glenn's story. It confirmed everything my mother had written. But what I still didn't understand was why Jack came east to find me.

"JT was just about destroyed by the death of James, then of Mary and the child," Glenn continued. "Took it real hard, as JT believed it was his duty, as the eldest, to go off and fight. I tried to reason with him that James had wanted to go and even fixed it so he *could* go, but JT was still heartbroken.

"When Robert announced *he* was going to enlist, I thought JT would hog-tie him to the bed posts to keep him on the ranch. But Robert was smart. Book-smart. That's how he got the nickname 'the Professor,' long before he ever got a job at any university. We were all in town one day, except Robert. He had one of his buddies drive him to Bozeman, and he enlisted. By the time JT found out, it was too late. The papers had been signed, and there was no getting out of the commitment.

"When Robert was sent to Chicago for training, JT got it into his head that Robert should woo your mother and bring her back to Montana. She was the closest living thing to James. Hell, old JT might have done it himself if'n he wasn't already married to Ida Mae." Seeing the disgusted look on my face, Glenn quickly added, "I know. It's disturbing. And believe me, Robert didn't want any part of it. But JT was very persuasive, and he wouldn't take no for an answer. I think that was JT's first attempt at using guilt to get his way.

"As it turned out, it was all for nothing. Your mother didn't have a lick of interest in Robert. Good thing for the both of them. Robert never intended on coming back to Montana after he returned from Korea. He went to a couple of different colleges on the GI Bill, and after he got all those letters after his name, he started teaching. JT worked on him for years to come teach in Bozeman. Even got the university president to offer Robert a job. But that wasn't enough to get him back to Montana. I guess Robert figured if he came back here to teach, he'd end up on the ranch, one way or another. He told me once that he'd seen enough cattle and shoveled enough horse shit to last a lifetime. No, ranch life wasn't for him. Hell, ranch life isn't for a lot of folks. Maybe it's not for you either, huh, Elizabeth?"

I didn't say anything. But I was certainly getting a better picture of JT.

"Years went by, and we all thought JT had given up on pursuing the connection with your mother. But as Jack got older, JT insisted that Robert find your mother and see how she fared. Robert did as he pleased. He didn't feel under any obligation to follow JT's orders. And more years went by. But for unknown reasons, Robert did finally make some inquiries, and surprisingly, he did locate your mother. And you.

"Once JT found out, he decided it was you that Jack would marry. Not just you, but how and when," Glenn told me. "Jack rebelled by delaying JT's orders to go back east. He rebelled by choosing Cathy. Now, one would think that JT would have welcomed a marriage binding the two ranches, but he had something against Cathy. He just didn't like her. Said she couldn't be trusted. Referred to her as 'the tramp' whenever he did talk about her. But old JT usually gets what he wants, and eventually Jack went east and stayed with the Professor."

I could only imagine that the look on my face was a result of my fears being confirmed: Jack *had* come looking for me. But if Glenn noticed it, he ignored it. As I mulled over this new reality, Glenn told me more.

"Jack was not too keen on marrying a *city* girl. An outsider, as he put it. But he had one look at you, and he felt something, he told me. He was physically attracted to you and, of course, he wanted to bed you. But not just for a fling. He wanted you for his wife. You know Jack could'a had any girl between here and Bozeman. He was extremely popular in college. When Jack returned to the ranch after Christmas, anyone could tell he was smitten. None of us are sure what exactly happened over the holidays, but he was Stetson-hat-over-cowboy-boots gone." Glenn chuckled at his own turn on the idiom. "As for the comment of *keeping it in the clan*, as Cathy put it, that stems from the long-ago rumors that Ida Mae, JT's wife, was some kind of cousin. No one ever knew for sure if she was or wasn't, and JT never would tell, but that's how the rumor about the Juddsons started."

I didn't know what to say. I knew from Mom's letter that a lot of what Glenn told me was true. *Was Jack truly "smitten," as Glenn said?*

"But Jack is stubborn, Elizabeth," Glenn disclosed. "Just like his old man. Jack doesn't know how to fix the problems right now between you two. He's a bit paralyzed—again, kinda like JT. Jack doesn't want to do anything that will make you leave him."

I *was* still in love with that sexy, seductive Montana man. My icy anger thawed slightly, and my heart once more longed for my cowboy. *Did it really matter how he found me?*

CHAPTER 23

I don't think either one of us knew how to end our "cold war." Jack continued to get up early and work late. The few times I was still awake and reading when he finally came up to bed, I didn't know how to start the conversation. I would silently beg him to say something. Anything to break the ice. But our polite frostiness continued.

I decided to make the first gesture. Gritting my teeth, I bundled up and headed over for breakfast in the big house. Conversation stopped when I walked into the dining room. On the way to my chair next to Jack's, running my hand across his back, I bent down and whispered in his ear, "Good morning, *darlin'*."

The look of surprise, then pleasure and hope, in his eyes nearly broke my heart.

The moment quickly passed when JT said, "Good morning, Elizabeth. You're a beautiful sight on this chilly morning." He sounded sincere, but then again, you never knew about old JT.

Sarah came in just then with toast and coffee, my usual

fare whenever I got up early enough to join the men.

As if my entrance wasn't a monumental moment in our marriage, the discussion turned right back to cattle and politics. Nixon had been reelected in November and inaugurated last month. Beef prices were up over last year. The *Farmer's Almanac* promised spring would be early this year.

The men lingered longer than usual over their coffee until JT cleared his throat, signaling work on the ranch should begin.

~~~~~~

Jack gently bussed Beth before he left. And he wasn't rejected. That spark of hope was all he needed to make some plans. Jack had asked Glenn for some advice a week or so ago. The idea they both agreed upon was to take Beth off the ranch for a getaway. Jack was sure if he could get her alone—and *under him* a few times—things would work out between them. He went ahead and made the reservations.

~~~~~~

Jack came back to the little house earlier than he had in weeks. I was reading. What else was there to do?

"Beth, we're going into Bozeman tomorrow," he announced.

"Tomorrow?" I asked him. "Who? You and Glenn? What for?"

"No, darlin'. You and me. We'll be away a couple of days. And *nights*," he added with a wink.

We still had a lot of air to clear, but my Jack-deprived body betrayed me, so I said, "Okay, I'll go pack."

~~~~~~

Jack almost told her not to pack much. He wasn't planning on leaving the hotel room the entire time. But he didn't want Beth to change her mind. So he just winked again.

~~~~~~

In the morning, the weather cooperated, which meant no new snow. Jack put our bags in one of the pickups and I started to hop in the cab.

"Here, Beth, this way." Jack gestured to one of the tractors.

With a boost from him, I climbed into the taller vehicle, and then watched as he jumped in and fired it up.

"We'll tow the truck with the tractor," he informed me.

I should have known by now not to question what he was doing, but with his uncanny sense to anticipate my questions, he assured me that he'd done this before. He didn't take the usual route off the ranch. Jack skirted the drifts, staying in the troughs where the wind had swept the snow clear, until we reached the county road.

"I'm leaving the tractor here. We'll probably need it to get back to the house," he told me.

~~~~~~

Beth blossomed the farther they got from the ranch and the closer they got to Bozeman. She snuggled up next to Jack on the truck's bench seat. Of course, she might have just been cold, trying to steal his warmth. But Jack didn't care about the reason. He had his woman, and they weren't leaving the hotel room until they had worked things out.

~~~~~~

After checking in at the Cattleman's, Jack let the bellboy take their bags up to the room. With his hand on Beth's back, he directed her toward the hotel bar.

"I could use a beer," he told her. "How about you?"

"Sounds good," Beth agreed.

At a small table in a quiet corner, each with a beer and sharing a bowl of peanuts, Jack wasn't sure how or where to start.

From her big purse, Beth pulled out a thick bundle of papers. Handing it to him, she said, "Read this."

~~~~~~

I watched him as he read my mother's letter.

"How long have you had this?" he asked.

"A long time. But I only just read it a few weeks ago," I confessed. Before he could ask anything else, I added, "And Glenn told me the rest. About JT's obsession with my mother and then with me."

Jack didn't say anything at first. But when he looked at me, I'd never seen his blue eyes look so sad. "I *did* come to Illinois to find you," he admitted. "That first night at Lucy's party, you were so much fun to talk to. But yet, you were so shy. I had thought to just tell you and let you dump me, so I could go back to JT and tell him, 'Well, I tried.' But I didn't want you to give me the boot. I wanted to get to know you better. And then at Christmas, I knew you weren't a virgin, but you might as well have been, never having had an orgasm," he said, lowering his voice. "I was *in love* with you before that, but I *loved you* then. I wanted to marry you and bring you to Montana."

I didn't know what to say. His honesty touched me. But before I could respond, he continued, "Beth, I know you want to leave. I know you're unhappy, and Montana is not what you had expected. But I love you. I don't want you to leave. Will you stay a little longer? Give ranch life, *and me*, another chance?"

I couldn't stand to see the hurt in Jack's eyes or to have this proud man beg. I ended his suffering, replying, "Yes, Jack, I will stay," as I reached across the small table and took his hand.

~~~~~~

Jack sensed that they were *both* looking forward to the make-up sex they so needed. He quickly signed the bar bill to their room and escorted Beth to the elevators. Stepping in and finding the car empty, he pressed the button for the top floor. As the elevator doors closed, Jack took Beth in his arms and kissed her passionately. Like a spark to dry kindling, it was all either of them needed to cling to each other, trying to meld their bodies together.

~~~~~~

The *ding* of the elevator indicating the doors were about to open made us briefly separate, but once inside our room, we picked up right where we left off. Jack had my coat off and my jeans unzipped in one quick movement. Tossing his coat and hat on the chair, he toed off his boots, watching me the entire time. *Is he still afraid I might bolt? Change my mind?* He squatted in front of me, lifted my jean-clad leg, causing me to grab his shoulder for balance, and tugged off my boot. After repeating the motion with the other boot, he stood and peeled off my jeans, then gave me a gentle nudge toward the king-sized bed.

Lying close to me with one possessive arm around me, he nuzzled my neck and nibbled my earlobe before he got serious. Kissing me, using his tongue to deepen the kiss, he had one hand under my shirt, trying to get to my nipple. With a frustrated grunt, he stopped the kiss only long enough to strip me of my top and flick the hook on my bra. With full access, there was no stopping his fondling. Soon my panties were damp and I could feel his hard shaft pushing up against my thigh. Snaking my hand between us, I tried to unsnap his jeans, but he grabbed my hand and said, "No, Beth. Not yet," and continued to tease me with his tongue and fingers.

Jack lavished kisses from my neck to my breasts. Not stopping there, he spent a few moments around my belly button, softly tickling me with his beard. Sliding my panties off, he continued his traveling kisses on my inner thighs to between my legs. Fingering me, finding me wet, Jack groaned. Or maybe it was a moan. But I nearly screamed when his lips and tongue found my delicate nub, suckling gently. The sensation was the most intense I'd ever felt. Reflexively, I lifted my hips to grant him deeper access. Accepting the challenge, he licked and probed and I crashed into a powerful orgasm. Feeling me go limp, he finally shucked off his jeans and shirt and slowly, gently pushed his eager shaft into me. I hadn't thought it was possible to experience that much pleasure, but I was sure wrong.

Afterward, lying together, our bodies entwined and our hearts closer than they'd been in weeks, Jack asked me again, "Beth, will you stay with me?"

I nodded, then, realizing he needed to hear the words, whispered, "Yes, Jack. I do love you. I will stay."

Rolling me over on top of him, Jack shouted a cowboy hee-haw to the ceiling.

"Now order me some room service, husband." With a raised eyebrow at my request and my tone, Jack opened his mouth to speak, but I quickly added, giggling, "I'm starving, darlin'."

~~~~~~

The weekend was just what we needed. We had some of the best sex to date. Between making love and room service, we talked about everything. I finally opened up to him about what was bothering me. I knew now that he had come looking for me, but that it didn't matter so much anymore. Maybe Glenn had told Jack about our talk in the barn. Maybe he hadn't. That didn't matter, either.

I hesitated to bring up Cathy, but since we were clearing the air, so to speak, I asked him again. "Jack, what is the history with you and Cathy? Why does she come to the ranch so often?"

"We were together, up until the time I came looking for you," Jack confessed. "But our relationship is over. In the past for me. She'd rather it not be."

I was sure he was waiting for a reaction, but I just thanked him for his honesty, which didn't deserve an argument. *I'll have to have a word with her this spring about staying away from my man.*

"I've visited the cemetery, Jack. I've seen the graves," I told him.

When Jack didn't say anything, I thought the subject was closed. Then he began, "My mother, Ida Mae, was not a strong woman. She was barely over five feet tall and rail-thin. And never very healthy. Doc Hardin called her 'sickly' one time, and JT pulled him aside, threatening bodily harm if Hardin ever called her that again."

Although I guessed this, Jack told me she had a lot of difficulty not just *getting* pregnant, but reaching full-term. All her other babies died within hours or months of their births. "I was the only healthy one," he sadly told me.

~~~~~~

Later in the weekend, I asked Jack, "Do you think Doc Hardin will give me any more birth control pills?"

"I doubt it, but we can ask."

I told him about my long-ago diagnosis of a tipped uterus and confessed it might make it difficult to get pregnant. I didn't want to tell him it might be *impossible* to conceive. We talked about whether we should tell JT. Then we decided not to and just let things take their course.

We agreed from now on to be honest with each other and share our feelings—well, I agreed. I wasn't sure Jack, being the tough cowboy, would tell me his *feelings*. But hopefully he would tell me more about himself.

I told him that I had found out from Glenn how JT ended up in the wheelchair. But I took Glenn's advice and didn't try to comfort or excuse Jack.

Jack did confide in me his hopes and dreams for the ranch. He talked about new procedures and got very animated about wanting to try some of them until he would remember that JT would never agree to it.

Monday morning, our last day in Bozeman, Jack said he had an errand to run and he'd be back soon. I took a long bath in the tub that could have easily accommodated several guests.

Feeling a bit sore but extremely satisfied, I wrapped myself in a soft, fluffy bathrobe and walked into the bedroom. There, in the middle of the bed, was a small gift-wrapped box.

"Open it," Jack told me with one of his devilish winks.

Inside was a plump gold heart. Just the charm, no chain. When I looked at him questioningly, he said, "It's to remind you, Beth, that you will *always* have my heart. Let's add it to your horseshoe necklace."

He turned me around and undid the clasp. Slipping the heart onto the chain, he briefly held it up for me to see before he refastened it.

"Happy Valentine's Day, darlin'," he whispered as he nuzzled my neck.

Those few days brought us closer together than we'd ever been. Hurt feelings were aired. Misunderstandings were cleared. Secrets were shared. On that long weekend, we made it back to where we were when we first came to the ranch.

~~~~~~

The weekend *was* a great idea. The sex was fabulous. Beth was uninhibited and spontaneous. She told Jack that she knew about JT's accident. She let him read a letter that her mother had left her. He wanted to tell her that it was on JT's orders that he *had* gone looking for her and that he hated JT for forcing him into it. But it was true that when he became so attracted to her and couldn't wait to get to know her better, he almost thanked JT. But Jack thought it was best to let the old man think his plan worked. It didn't matter to Jack. He loved Beth with his heart and soul, regardless of what JT wanted. Beth was no longer so upset about how they met, and Jack was relieved.

One day a couple of weeks ago, Jack had seen Glenn go into the barn when he knew Beth was grooming Buttercup. Glenn was in there for some time, but when Jack asked him about it, Glenn mumbled something and then, in typical Glenn fashion, changed the subject with a question about the busted manure spreader.

But the most surprising revelation...just last night Beth had told him she had a medical condition that might make it difficult to get pregnant. Interesting how she decided to share that when her pills were running out. *Doc Hardin never said anything about a condition, and the old fool had examined her, right?*

~~~~~~

In March, the weather finally moderated. There would be a couple of really warm days, and the snow melted quickly. Within two weeks, most of the snow was gone. There were, of course, a few huge drifts by some of the buildings, especially on the north side, that stubbornly refused to melt.

By the end of March, the weather was breaking. Even the short sunny days warmed the earth and teased the grass to a pale green. It was time to start moving the cattle away from the ranch. Over many breakfasts in the big house, JT, Glenn, and Jack would discuss the best area to start with. Glenn and Jack had done some riding over the last few weeks, checking out fences and grazing areas. If only they knew where the bear had wintered. If it *even was* a bear. Calving was right around the corner. *And NO, JT, Beth is not pregnant yet.*

After the weekend in Bozeman, things between Jack and Beth had improved, and he was itching to take her riding again. It would be nice to get back to the routine of their early days on the ranch. Making love at noon and again at bedtime. Winter had kept Cathy marooned on her own ranch, thank God.

~~~~~~

It was late afternoon when one of the ranch hands came racing up to the barn.

"Frank shot the bear! Frank got the bear! Come quick," Russ hollered to Jack and Glenn.

Russ and Frank had been out a distance from the ranch, watching over a small bunch of cattle they had moved a few days before. Because the men were out of walkie-talkie range with the homestead, Russ galloped back right after Frank had taken the shot and the bear was down.

Glenn and Jack quickly mounted up, following Russ. When

they got to Frank, he was on his knees, doubled over, moaning something terrible. *Shit!* Had the shot not killed the bear and Frank had gotten mauled? Frank, bear fur, and cow guts were tangled together, so it was hard to tell. But when they got closer, they could see it wasn't a bear at all. It was Cathy in that damn fur coat. And Frank had shot her. Dead. *Oh, fuck.*

In Cathy's hand was a ten-inch Bowie hunting knife, covered in blood, which she had used to slice open the cow from forelegs to ass. *Dammit, Cathy. Fucking crazy bitch. Killing our cattle!* No wonder no other ranchers had been having this problem. This was her way of getting even with him.

It was easy to see how Frank mistook Cathy for the bear. She had been hunched over the cow and in that coat...well, from a distance, it did look like a bear savaging that poor animal. The only odd thing was the rest of the small herd had just kept grazing close by. Had it really been a bear, the herd would be restless, on the move away from the danger. This unfortunate bovine had wandered or been lured from the herd for this nefarious deed.

~~~~~~

Old JT took Cathy's death hard. He never particularly liked her. He often called her a tramp. He'd made it clear many times that there was no way Jackson would marry her. JT told him over and over again to use protection if he just had to fuck her.

But the fact that a friend, a neighbor, would *mutilate* his cows hit JT hard. And that she derived some sick pleasure in doing it, all because of her jealousy of Elizabeth... JT just shook his head.

Both the sheriff and the coroner ruled her death as an accident, but Frank still carried a ton of guilt. Once the story got out, however, everyone said Cathy had gotten what she deserved.

~~~~~~

Spring finally came with sunny skies and warm temperatures. The snow was all gone. The grazing areas were green and lush. Cattle had been moved away from the ranch. The cycle of ranch life was starting over. Any day now the heifers would be dropping their calves.

Things between Jack and Beth were good. He would take her riding several times a week. Jack knew she'd figured out that he was looking for calves and checking the fences, but she didn't mind. They made love often, but no baby yet, even though she was off the pill. Maybe that tipped uterus was making it difficult, but it sure was fun trying.

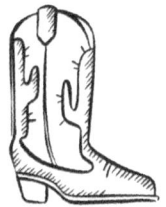

EPILOGUE

I've been on the ranch for four years now. We have three sons: John Jr., Michael, and James. Yes, all named for the Juddson men: grandfather and uncles.

When I finally got pregnant with JJ, as we call him, I worried that his entire life was already plotted out. He'd be expected to live and work on the ranch, whether that was his calling or not. Lucky for everyone, I had *three* sons. I hoped at least one of them would love the ranch the way Jack does. The others can follow their passions. Or stay. But they all will have a choice.

JT died after Michael was born. It was as if he had been waiting to make sure another generation was coming along to keep things going. All those years in the wheelchair finally caught up with him. He never followed any of Doc Hardin's warnings to watch his weight and get some exercise. Everyone knew he had enough money to install some exercise equipment; hell, he could even have built an indoor pool. He died in his sleep, alone.

After JT passed, Jack and I, with our two sons, moved into the big house. Changes have been made over the years.

Gradually. Some bright yellow throw pillows on the big old leather chairs brightened up that dreary living room. I was able to remove a lot of the old ranch tools on the pretext that our boys could get hurt by them. Jack was eager to hang the framed Charles Russell prints I purchased. Our favorites were *Wagon Boss* and *Roping a Wolf*. I tried not to take away all the masculinity, but instead insert some softness. In the spring, I set out a vase or two of cut daffodils from the bulbs I had planted the year before JJ was born. Jack approved.

Initially, I shared the cooking with Sarah, working in some of my mom's recipes. With Ruby's help with the boys, I could even do some baking.

I did learn there was a pattern to moving the herds in the summer, so that one area did not get over-grazed and so that the cattle were closer to the ranch by fall. I even went out on a drive a couple of times. I think Michael might have been conceived when Jack made love to me in some tall grass in the middle of a lazy afternoon.

Glenn became a great uncle. I mean an *excellent* uncle. But I made him promise not to ever tell the boys the story about how Jack and I met. That was a family secret that was buried with old JT.

"Aunt" Lucy comes to Montana every summer and stays a couple of weeks. We try to plan it when Jack is busy moving the herds so we can have some girl time.

Every Christmas Eve, Jack gives me one present to open. It is always the latest bestseller.

I did become a better rider, but I was nowhere near talented enough to guide the herd or chase strays. I did find a rapport with the chuck wagon cook, and he let me help him from time to time.

I appreciate the land and that it's been in the family for generations. I've come to be in awe of the raw beauty of this part of our country. Isolated? Yes. Rugged? Yes. It's not for everyone. Truthfully, if it wasn't for that handsome, blue-eyed cowboy who swept me off my feet, it wouldn't be for me. But I love him with my whole being and can't imagine being anywhere but here, with him and our boys.

I smile to myself every time I reach for my boots. They are all broken in now. And oh, so comfortable. *And so am I.*

Acknowledgments

Writing a book is hard work and it's easy to get discouraged and want to quit. I will be forever grateful for my best friend, editor extraordinaire and tireless cheerleader, Deborah Fransen, for encouraging me to always keep going. The early day of brainstorming in Indiana were invaluable to me. Your subsequent emails, texts and phone calls along with the motivational greeting cards and sticky notes were truly appreciated. And of course, your editing skills made this book so much better. Words cannot express how thankful I am for your friendship.

To the Beta Readers–Barb, Leigh Ann, Bonnie, Katrina Kreider, JK and Brenna–thank you for taking the time to read my book and offer excellent suggestions for improvement. I sincerely appreciated your help in making this book better. And I hope you'll be willing to read the next one!

Thanks to Jenny Tangles for the horseback riding advice. Any mistakes are all my own.

Thanks to Cal at the UPS Store, for your encouraging words and your help with the beta copies.

To the team at Atmosphere Press–Nick Courtright, Alex Kale, Megan Sells, Erin Larson, Cassandra Felten, Dakota Reed, Claire Denson, Elana Sederholm, Ronaldo Alves, and Matthew Fielder–thank you for your help and guidance on this journey. I know this was not *your* first rodeo, but being mine I couldn't have asked for a better team! I truly appreciated how responsive everyone was to all my questions. The support and encouragement along the way was outstanding.

To all the people who have chosen to read my book, I

hope like Beth, that I've taken you briefly to Montana. And to those who might read this and *live* in Montana, please forgive me for any fictionalization of your beautiful state. Any mistakes about Montana or ranching are all my own.

And lastly to Mac. Although you've never read a romance novel and most likely will not read this one, thank you for your encouragement, your patience with my writing schedule and deadlines, and your outstanding tech support.

About Atmosphere Press

Founded in 2015, Atmosphere Press was built on the principles of Honesty, Transparency, Professionalism, Kindness, and Making Your Book Awesome. As an ethical and author-friendly hybrid press, we stay true to that founding mission today.

If you're a reader, enter our giveaway for a free book here:

SCAN TO ENTER
BOOK GIVEAWAY

If you're a writer, submit your manuscript for consideration here:

SCAN TO SUBMIT
MANUSCRIPT

And always feel free to visit Atmosphere Press and our authors online at atmospherepress.com. See you there soon!

About the Author

SAM LAMB is a retired university accountant, who splits the year residing in Illinois, Missouri and Texas. Besides writing, hobbies include traveling, photography, swimming and biking. Sam's quieter activities are reading and binging Netflix.

Contact Sam at samlamb325@gmail.com
Follow Sam on Facebook at Samlamb325

www.ingramcontent.com/pod-product-compliance
Lightning Source LLC
LaVergne TN
LVHW041932070526
838199LV00051BA/2782